PRAISE FOR

A *School Library Journal* Best Book of the Year

★ "Magoon makes space for and celebrates the
sensitive and solitary middle-grade readers who
are happiest flying under the radar."
—*Shelf Awareness*, starred review

"Taking great care with issues related to blended
families and bullying, Magoon gives readers
another emotional and satisfying read."
—*The Horn Book*

"Engrossing and heartwarming;
explores belonging, love, and forgiveness in
families and friendships."
—*Kirkus Reviews*

"A wacky adventure that toes
the line between playful fantasy and
deep-rooted emotional journey."
—*School Library Journal*

ALSO BY KEKLA MAGOON

Camo Girl

Rebellion of Thieves

Reign of Outlaws

The Rock and the River

The Season of Styx Malone

Shadows of Sherwood

Infinity Riders (Voyagers, Book 4)

CHESTER KEENE CRACKS THE CODE

KEKLA MAGOON

A YEARLING BOOK

Text copyright © 2022 by Kekla Magoon
Cover art copyright © 2022 by Charlot Kristensen

All rights reserved. Published in the United States by Yearling, an imprint of Random House Children's Books, a division of Penguin Random House LLC, New York. Originally published in hardcover in the United States by Wendy Lamb Books, an imprint of Random House Children's Books, a division of Penguin Random House LLC, New York, in 2022.

Yearling and the jumping horse design are registered trademarks of Penguin Random House LLC.

Visit us on the Web! rhcbooks.com

Educators and librarians, for a variety of teaching tools, visit us at RHTeachersLibrarians.com

The Library of Congress has cataloged the hardcover edition of this work as follows:
Names: Magoon, Kekla, author.
Title: Chester Keene cracks the code / Kekla Magoon.
Description: First edition. | New York: Wendy Lamb Books, [2022] | Audience: Ages 8–12. | Audience: Grades 4–6. | Summary: Eleven-year-old Chester and his classmate Skye, tasked with a complex puzzle-solving mission, discover the key to their spy assignment is to stop a heist, but cracking the code could mean finding out things are not always what they seem.
Identifiers: LCCN 2021030986 (print) | LCCN 2021030987 (ebook) | ISBN 978-1-5247-1599-1 (hardcover) | ISBN 978-1-5247-1600-4 (library binding) | ISBN 978-1-5247-1601-1 (ebook)
Subjects: CYAC: Treasure hunt (Game)—Fiction. | Schools—Fiction. | Single-parent families—Fiction.
Classification: LCC PZ7.M2739 Ch 2022 (print) | LCC PZ7.M2739 (ebook) | DDC [Fic]—dc23

ISBN 978-1-5247-1602-8 (paperback)

Printed in the United States of America
10 9 8 7 6 5 4 3 2 1
First Yearling Edition 2023

Random House Children's Books supports the First Amendment and celebrates the right to read.

Penguin Random House LLC supports copyright. Copyright fuels creativity, encourages diverse voices, promotes free speech, and creates a vibrant culture. Thank you for buying an authorized edition of this book and for complying with copyright laws by not reproducing, scanning, or distributing any part in any form without permission. You are supporting writers and allowing Penguin Random House to publish books for every reader.

FOR SAMMY

ROUTINE

Everyone probably assumes my life is very boring. Strictly speaking, they're not wrong. It's really just that I like things to be done a certain way.

I get up in the morning at 6:35, five minutes after my alarm goes off at 6:30. I have to take five minutes to just lie there and look at the ceiling. I'm not sure why.

A lot of thoughts fill my mind in that morning quiet, and the first thing I want to do is find a way to not think them. When my snooze alarm goes off, it plays music, which helps. My brain sings along to *The Best of Motown* and that's always a good way to get things going.

"Things" being: my morning routine.

First, the shower. I wash my hair in there every other day. Brush teeth, for bad-breath control. Put on clothes, usually jeans. I own one pair of corduroys, but I only wear them maybe every other week. Just to mix it up. On top, it's either T-shirts, or polos with various stripes across the chest. The T-shirts feel better, but the polos do look quite a bit nicer. It all depends on whether it's a day to be comfortable or a little more stylish. On the rare occasions when I do polo *and* corduroys . . . look out world, here comes Chester Keene.

By 6:55, I'm ready to roll. I scoot into the living room, plop my backpack by the door, with five minutes to spare, which is exactly how long it takes to log in on Mom's computer and check my email. Fingers crossed.

Today, the only new email is something from school about Yearbook Club. Nothing from Dad.

Refresh.

Still nothing. It has been over two weeks since he last wrote me back.

New message.

Dad? Is everything OK?

My fingers hang over the keys. There isn't much else to say.

Please write me back.

Wait. Am I being overanxious? Needy? Impatient?
Delete.

He'll get back to me when he can. I'm sure of it. Two weeks really isn't that long, considering we haven't seen each other in eight and a half years. Knowing what I know now, though, I can't help but worry. What if he's in danger, or—

Mom's bedroom door opens. Her slippers shuffle against the carpet.

Stealth mode: activate!

By the time she emerges from the hallway, wrapped in her fuzzy green bathrobe, the computer is dark and quiet and I'm at the kitchen counter pouring a bowl of cereal.

"Hi, Mom!" My big morning smile is ready to go.

"Mmm-hmm." Mom kisses my forehead. The coffeepot is timed to start sizzling right about now, and it does. I milk up my Honey Nut Cheerios as Mom watches the coffee drip, drip, drip.

Observation: Mom has on a fresh coat of nail polish, already dry and shining. She must have done it last night. She's chosen the giant Niagara Falls mug, which means she's extra tired this morning.

We sit across from each other in silence, Mom sniffing coffee steam and me crunching away. Mom has this look on her face, the one that means she's thinking hard about something.

"How's my Chester this morning?" she says, once the caffeine starts to kick in.

"I'm fine, Mom." There are other things I could say, but I won't. The thing about Mom is that she worries a lot. Once on the phone to her friend Amanda, when she thought I was asleep, Mom said that raising me alone is really stressful. So I try hard not to give her any more problems. I can handle things myself, and when I need advice, I can always ask Dad. He might be slow at email, but he's really smart.

"That's good," Mom answers. "And if you're ever not fine, you keep me posted, okay?"

"Of course." But my smile isn't quite enough reassurance, I can tell. She really does worry A LOT.

At 7:16, it's time to move.

The last of the Honey Nut Cheerios milk goes down like sweet nectar. Yum. I pop my bowl into the dishwasher and head to the door.

Sneakers, jacket, backpack on. I whisper my checklist while Mom stands in the kitchen doorway, lightly fanning her second cup of coffee with gentle breaths.

"Homework, check. Gym clothes, check. Lunch card, check."

"Got everything?" Mom says, which is part of the routine.

Spy gear, check.

"Yep." The silent addition is not for Mom's ears. It's our secret, Dad's and mine.

OBSERVATION, CONCLUSION

The walk to the bus stop takes two minutes. One minute to walk along the balcony and down the stairs from our second-floor apartment, through the parking lot and out the driveway, and a whole other minute to go all the way down the sidewalk to the second driveway entrance to our apartment complex.

It's weird. I'm the only kid that gets picked up at this location, but the stop is still all the way on the other side. Mom says they simply haven't updated the routes in a few years. There's a kid on the other side that used to ride this bus, but he's in high school now.

I have a plan, though. Every day I stand a few yards closer to my side of the complex. I figure the bus driver isn't looking for the driveway itself, he's looking for the kid that needs to get picked up. So I'm thinking I can train him over time to just pick me up at my own driveway. So far, so good.

When the process is done, I'll be able to leave the house one minute later. I don't know yet what I'll do with the extra time. Linger over the Cheerios? Lie in bed for six minutes? Maybe I could start wearing a belt or some sort of accessory. That might use up some time.

Observation: Mrs. O'Leary's car is not in its spot. She goes to yoga class on Thursday, but it's Friday. Interesting. There is a city work crew opening a manhole on the next block. Sewer work? Mr. Carson didn't clean up after his dog this morning, and he's usually very diligent. His sciatica must be acting up.

The bus ride itself is a jouncy, bouncy, jaw-rattling experience. My row is the fourth up from the back, so we get extra height flying over all the potholes. I slouch down low and prop my knees up on the seat back in front of me. No one ever sits with me, so I put my backpack next to me and hook my arm through the straps so it doesn't bounce off the seat. I prefer the corners of my textbooks not get dented.

Observation: Marla's braces bands are a new color. She's been to the orthodontist. Kevin is wearing the same pants with that ketchup stain on the knee that he's been wearing for three days. Maybe their washing machine is broken. The gas station on the corner finally fixed the typo in their lettered sign. For two weeks it has read, *By 1 get 1 free Pizza buy the slice.* Guess someone finally pointed out the error.

Keen observation skills are a hallmark of effective spy-craft. The history of espionage book Dad sent for my birthday tells all about it. You have to know everything, see everything. Observation, conclusion. Observation, conclusion. When you make an observation and can't make a conclusion, and you're left with more questions, you have to keep observing. Information is power. A small detail can tell an entire story.

It's too bouncy to write on the bus, so once I get to school, I will add all these notes to my spy notebook from Dad. Making the notes is a key part of my training, and it also makes me feel closer to him, even though he's far away.

Dad's a real spy. He can't come right out and say that, of course, but he's given me enough clues that I've figured it out. The gifts he sends, for Christmas and my birthday, often have something to do with espionage. When I was smaller he sent LEGO sets and other random things, of course, but lately the theme is pretty clear. Binoculars, brain teaser games and logic puzzles, a lockpick practice set, *The Knowhow Book of Spycraft,* a utility belt with some cool gadgets, and the notebook and the history book, which is basically a training manual.

Dad's always been pretty clever about keeping his life a secret from me and Mom. His work makes him very busy, which is why he can't come visit. We don't even know where he lives, because it seems like he's always on the move. His packages come from all over the place. I started investigating them over a year ago, and nothing. This summer, though, he slipped up.

The packing slip from my birthday present box had a sender's email address. It took me a month to get up the nerve, but I finally emailed Dad.

I had to send a lot of messages before he wrote back the first time. He must have been on a spy mission. But once I started writing him, I couldn't stop. There are a lot of guy things that it's hard to talk to Mom about, especially since I don't want her to worry. When things are bad at school, or when I'm sad or confused, I still have to be strong for Mom. And Dad gets that. It's been great having him to talk to.

For Christmas he sent the utility belt, and it felt like he was telling me it's time to step up my game. In his last email, he wrote:

> I'm proud of you, Chester. Keep doing what
> you're doing, and you'll be ready for anything the
> world throws at you.

So, I'm doing it. Observation, conclusion. Practicing my skills. I may only be a spy-in-training, but it's very important that I keep myself in top shape. Someday, Dad may need my help with a mission. And if that day comes, you better believe I'll be ready.

UNDER THE RADAR,
A STONE IN THE RIVER

There are benefits to going it alone in the cinder block jungle. All of the social pressure that everyone talks about in relation to school is simply not there if you never, ever talk to anyone.

Sure, people will say things from time to time, and sometimes those things are not very nice, but Dad says there are always going to be those people. And it turns out it's actually true: if you genuinely don't care what people think of you, then they actually end up thinking pretty highly of you. Occasionally there's a group project or something, but I'm good in school, so people don't mind teaming up with me. It's me who minds. I'm the one who wants to be left alone.

They don't understand me. I don't understand them. And none of us makes any effort to have it be otherwise. In the lunchroom sometimes, when everyone else is talking and laughing and having a nice time, I do wonder what that might feel like. In elementary school, things were easier. We had assigned seats for everything, even lunch. There were always people to play with and the other kids never seemed to mind me so much. But in middle school, everything is different. It's like there's a secret code that everyone knows but me, for how to get along and how to make friends. But I'm okay on my own. It's really okay. Spies are supposed to stay under the radar, after all. And I'd rather have nothing than have to deal with—

Someone slams into my back, sending my armful of books sprawling to the floor. "Go home and die, loser!"

Case in point.

Marc Ruffnagle towers over me. He grins from within his perpetual five-o'clock shadow. *It's not even nine a.m., jerkface!* is what I want to shout. Except I've learned that no one understands my insults anyway, so there is no point. Marc drifts away, picked up by the hallway current. Jerk. He's a head taller than everyone else, with shoulders like a brick column. He grunts more than he talks.

I bend over to pick up my stuff. Marc's long gone. He might not have even been talking to me. Hard to say. The stream of students parts around me, like a stone in a river. Steady. No one steps on me.

Perhaps I'm not even a stone, but a pebble. So insignificant as to not even be noticed.

Spycraft means blending in, not standing out, I remind myself.

I'd like to say the Marc encounter was an anomaly. Not the norm. But I can shake it off. I always do. Dad wrote once:

> The right thing to do is ignore him. No matter
> how hard it is. That's the only response that
> works on bullies that doesn't sink you to their
> level.

So I try not to even look Marc's way. Behind his back, the girls giggle and call him Marc Ruffalo, after that old actor guy that Mom thinks is hot. Marc Ruffian would be more accurate, though.

When I stand up, I become part of the hallway river again, just like that. As if nothing ever happened.

My homeroom desk is in the far back corner, completely by alphabetical coincidence. It's glorious. Having a K name usually lands me smack in the middle, surrounded. Is this how the Zs of the world usually feel, and if so, why do they complain so much to get teachers to mix up the rows? This is perfect.

As soon as my butt hits the seat, my notebook is in my

hand. Whenever I need it, I can pull it out and remember that I have a higher purpose.

Observation: Marc has possibly grown an inch. Also, he needs to apply more deodorant. Conclusion: Marc is either not too bright or has a damaged sense of smell; the personal hygiene learning curve is not that steep.

Observation: A whiff of chemicals from the linoleum. The hallway floor has been freshly waxed.

Adding my observations from earlier, too, fills up an entire page. That's great. Even in a moment of duress, I managed to have my spy senses working.

A smile sneaks across my face. A sore wrist and elbow is not the end of the world. I do have a higher purpose. Something Marc Ruff-n-tumble could never understand.

THE FRIDAY NIGHT
REIGN OF GLORY

After school, I ride the same bus home, except I get off two stops early and walk through the shopping center parking lot to a low, sprawling stone building that's set apart from the rest of the mall. Above the door hangs a neon sign that blinks with no discernible rhythm: BOWL.

Mom's best friend, Amanda, is the owner and manager here. She watches me until Mom gets off work. Monday through Thursday, I'm allowed to bowl for free after I finish my homework. But Friday is the best day at the bowling alley.

At four p.m. every Friday, Ralph comes in and opens up the laser tag arena for the weekend, and I get to compete for top scores. I can get three rounds in before Mom comes to get me at five-thirty. Currently I'm in third place, behind someone called THUNDR and a little punk called CHIKIN. I've never met THUNDR, but they must be actually good. They've held the top score as long as I've been playing. CHIKIN is this annoying seven-year-old who has no sense of sportsmanship. The only reason he wins is that he's so small he can fit into this one crevice on the side of the central tower. He hunkers in there and shoots everybody who walks by. Meanwhile, no one can reach him because he sits with his knees up over his vest.

My laser tag handle is CHESTY. I've thought about copying THUNDR and changing it to CHESTR, but misspelling goes against my sensibility.

"Hi, Amanda," I call out. She's busy dusting the floor around the ball return on Lane 17. She wields the big gray dust mop like she's grooving with a skinny, skinny partner. The sound system pumps out the Rock of the Eighties and Nineties mix: "I Wanna Dance with Somebody."

"Hey, Ches," she calls back. "How was school?"

"Same old!" I zip straight into her office and leave her to cleaning/crooning.

To say Amanda "watches" me is a bit loose. Her job keeps her very busy, so basically she makes sure I arrive and put my backpack somewhere safe, and she sets up a lane for me anytime I want to bowl. In between, I'm supposed to stay in her office and do my homework, but she doesn't really notice or care if I decide to take a jaunt over to the mall, or to the park, or whatnot. It's not like I really need a babysitter. It's a technicality. There's some rule that says eleven-year-olds can't go home after school on their own. Next year, I won't have to be babysat, even for pretend.

First things first, pop over to Amanda's computer. Inbox: zero. Sigh.

It's only three, so there's still an hour before laser tag. Maybe a bit of fresh air would be nice.

Amanda is rocking hard with the dust mop to "I'd Do Anything for Love." She doesn't notice me leaving the office or heading out the door. It's fine.

Usually I go over to the mall, because there's no better place to people-watch and make observations. But today I just do a loop around the parking lot, heading for the main road on the far side of the mall.

This area has a more industrial feeling. The automotive department from the big-box store juts out from the mall, and standing alone opposite that is the Honeycomb Storage Solutions warehouse. They rent out storage spaces on one side of the building and the other side is a store selling garage shelves and plastic bins and things like that. The most direct route to my favorite spot carries me right under their giant beehive-shaped sign.

The industrial feeling is enhanced because Alexander Street starts tilting upward into a bridge over the river at this point, so there's a bit of a feeling of being under the expressway or down by the docks. Not that there are any actual docks—it's not that big of a river. But on the opposite bank, train tracks run along the river toward the central train station about a mile away. Part of the city's walk-jog-bike trail runs between the water and the tracks, too, so the bridge is pretty long.

The Alexander Street Bridge gets a lot of traffic, but it has a nice wide pedestrian walkway that is separated from the cars by a fence. A few bikers and walkers zip past me but I'm taking my own sweet time. I draw deep breaths of the freshwater air, feeling the thrum and hum of cars sending tremors through the bridgework.

The best view is from the middle of the bridge. Water below, sky above, trees lining the banks where the river curves out of sight in the near distance. The railing is chest-high, but if I lean into it just a bit and tune out the sound of the traffic, it feels like I'm suspended in the sky over the water.

Observation: The water is calm. There must not have been any boats in a while. The jogger lady in the red suit crosses the bridge a few minutes earlier than usual. Did she leave early, or is she improving her time? Two men in business suits speak animatedly to each other as they approach. Is it a meeting run overtime, or mutual complaining about their boss? Complaining.

If I had more time, I might wander over to the riverside trail and sit on one of the benches. Sometimes there are ducks.

I might sit and close my eyes and listen as the afternoon trains chug by. Hold perfectly still and absorb their sound, smell their steam, feel their rumble. The trains have a familiar rhythm, the soothing mechanical hum of a well-oiled engine and people getting to where they need to go at the exact time they need to be there. They're perfect.

When I stroll back up to the bowling alley, Amanda's taking out the trash. She comes out the back door as I'm rounding toward the front.

"Chester?" she says, tossing the bags into the dumpster. "What are you doing?"

"Just a brief constitutional," I answer. That's a fancy word for taking a walk. Grown-ups will forgive a lot if you subtly remind them how smart and well-behaved you generally are.

Sure enough, Amanda smiles. "Constitutional, eh?"

"I wanted some fresh air. Sorry."

"No worries, kiddo." She ruffles my hair and squeezes my shoulder. I try to ignore the fact that those hands were just touching the garbage bin. "All done with homework? Want me to set up a lane for you?"

"Nah. Laser tag."

"Right."

The back door is exit only, so Amanda joins me on my path around the building. We wave to Chet, the teller at the E-Z Check Cashing Center across the way. I feel a little bad for Chet. His storefront is one massive pane of glass. He sits in a little cage inside the store and everyone can see him.

Chet waves back. He slides down from his high stool and exits his cage. He props open the store's front door by reaching up and pushing a little metal tab against the springs. "Hey," he says as we pass.

"Hey," we say back.

"You good?" Amanda adds. It's rare to see Chet outdoors.

"Yup." Chet motions down the alley. "It's the witching hour."

An armored bank truck lumbers around the corner. The regular cash delivery. Chet shuffles the ring of keys in his fist. The bank truck is pretty big up close. The two guys driving it look like they mean business.

I wonder what it's like to be in charge of a whole lot of money. The most cash I've ever held at one time was forty-two dollars, and I clutched it tight the whole time to keep from losing it. Maybe working in a cage makes Chet feel safe.

Amanda ushers me back inside the bowling alley. It's almost four, so I scoot straight over to the laser tag arena. Ralph is at the counter taking payments from the small crowd of players. I lurk at the back, since I don't have to sign up. He always saves me a spot.

The unexpected voice in my ear is all too familiar. "Well, if it isn't our friendly neighborhood loser."

Hot breath, BO. I don't even need to turn around to know. Don't want to. No choice, though.

Marc Ruff-n-ready and two of his primate friends are here, waiting in line for laser tag.

5

IN THE ARENA

Seeing Marc in the bowling alley turns my knees to jelly. Worlds colliding, the thing I've been looking forward to the most invaded by the person I dread most. This has never happened before.

"Hi, Marc." The bright spin on my voice surprises us both. "Hi, guys."

Marc's eyes narrow and he's about to speak, when the arena doors creak open, ominous music from the speakers inviting us in.

"Chester, just in time," Ralph says, stepping around the counter. He's a big, tall man and he always has my back. I smile at Marc. What can he do to me here?

When I'm in the arena, nothing can touch me. Not even Marc Ruff-puff-pastry.

"Friends of yours?" Ralph says, barely hiding the surprise in his voice. He should know better. Since when do I show up with friends?

"Oh, yeah," Marc says, throwing his arm around my shoulder and noogieing my head too hard. "Keene and us go way back."

It's obvious what's about to happen next. But there's no way to stop it. Ralph isn't the sort of guy you can count on to read a silent-but-desperate look.

"That's great, Chester. Why don't the four of you start off the blue team?"

"Blue's the best!" Marc crows. "Boo-yah!" The trio charges ahead of me.

"How's the competition look?" I ask Ralph.

"Noobs," he says. "It'll be a cakewalk." He sticks out his hand and I slap him five.

We pass through the door into the staging area. The lights are dim, to get our pupils dilated in preparation for the even darker arena. One wall of the black-painted room holds racks of glowing vests. The opposite side is where the players sit.

We clamber up onto the blue-painted section of the built-in steps. Resigned to my fate for the next twenty-five minutes, I sit quietly contemplating my game strategy. I could ditch Marc and friends in the arena, no problem. But would it make more sense to show them my skills? If they let me, I could help them learn. A glimmer of excitement trills inside me.

Maybe this is my chance to prove myself, a path to gaining their respect.

When I blink back into focus, Ralph is negotiating teams. There's a group of five that want to play together, and a group of three that want to play together, plus Marc and friends and me. The numbers aren't working out.

"I'll move," I offer. That will even things out. Marc's three plus the other three versus the group of five and me. Six on six. An even game.

Ralph feels bad about separating me from my "friends," I can tell. "There's always next round," I whisper to him as I cross over to Red. "Paying customers come first." This happens all the time, and as a solo player it's basically my job to go wherever I'm needed.

One of the guys on my new team has played before. His handle is SCHISM. He's not great, but not terrible. I can work with this.

Ralph drones through the rules briefing that I've heard a couple hundred times. Lights on the shoulders, chest, back, and laser gun. Must have both hands on the gun at all times or it won't fire. No running. Stand in one place and yell "Gamemaster!" over and over if you need help.

When I glance back at Marc, he points two fingers at me and crooks his thumb like he's pulling a trigger. *Get ready to die,* he mouths.

The correct response is to smile. Now my strategy is

crystal clear: Seek and destroy. I might as well have been born with a laser tag vest on. Marc doesn't know what he's in for.

—○

Ralph pushes the button that opens the double doors. The arena yawns in greeting. Inside, it's dark, cool, and cloudy with wisps of fake smoke. The laser-eyed sentinel at the top of the area blinks coolly at us. The best team strategy is to go straight to the top and hold the citadel, which of course is what Marc and friends immediately try to do.

"Dang it," says SCHISM. "We can take it back from them."

I say, "Eventually. First we should each take Blue base a couple of times."

"Whatever, kid," he says, and moves off with his friends toward the ramp. It's okay. I'm used to people assuming I don't know what I'm talking about.

All my red team members follow SCHISM, which is to be expected. I move through the mist smoothly, knowing exactly where I'm going.

On the ground level, there's a Red base in one corner and a Blue base in the other corner. You get more points at once for taking the sentinel, but if the other team is ignoring their base, it's easy to make up those points there. If you stand in the right spot—which I always do—you can take shots at the team up in the tower while waiting for the ground base to reactivate.

Pow. Pow. Pow. Boom. Moves like lightning. Five minutes in and I haven't even been hit yet.

Suddenly SCHISM slides in beside me. Perhaps he realized the wisdom of my advice. He shoots out Blue base next, then we wait for the sensor to light up again. This time, it's mine.

"Time to storm the citadel?" he whispers.

I nod. "Let's get 'em."

My score in the first game is rarely the best, because I need time to warm up. Today, though, I'm motivated.

SCHISM is a slightly better player than I thought, which helps. The two of us sneak up the winding ramp, taking out the enemy one by one. We snag the sentinel twice each along the way. We snake it right out from under them, even though they're all clustered in the citadel like they own the place.

I'll say this for Marc Ruff-around-the-edges: he doesn't know when to quit. They should've bailed out of there ages ago, but they think having the high ground means they're in charge. They're crowing like kings, but they're really sitting ducks.

"Like taking candy from a baby," SCHISM mutters.

"Only better," I answer. *Pow. Pow. Boom.*

6

DOWN TO EARTH

When I'm in the arena, nothing can touch me. But the victory goes to my head a bit.

I blow over the tip of my laser gun like the heroes do in the movies. I dominated. There's no question. I stride out of the fog, with my head high, straight into the bright-seeming light of the lobby. Do I even need to look at the score? Not really.

"Not so fast, Keene." Marc grabs my shirt.

His grip is tight, but not tight enough to stop the words from slipping out of me. "How do ya like me now?"

I don't know what came over me, talking back. You don't talk back. Period.

Marc tugs my shirt and then we're tripping, gliding, tumbling toward the arcade. In the shadowy triangle between the

Bling King claw game, the Whack-a-Mole, and the change machine, out of sight of the desk, the lanes, and the entrance to the arena, he strikes.

POW.

A flash of color bursts behind my eyelids. My ears ring with a tinkling sound, or maybe the force of my body being slammed into the change machine knocked a few quarters loose.

I've been pushed, shoved, kicked, knocked down, teased, called names, and threatened, but I've never been punched. My body is not made of glass, and I know this, but inside me, a layer of something shatters. The pieces rain down, down, down, as I slide into a crouch against the corner.

Standing over me, Marc says something I can't decipher, in a tone I'll never forget.

And then I'm alone again. Untucking my head from the crook of my arm takes an act of will. The cheerful blinking lights of the arcade games taunt me. The cartoon whack-a-mole, cowering beneath the big scary hammer, seems to gaze down upon me with sympathy.

Dad wrote once:

> If ignoring him doesn't work, you'll have to stand
> up to him. Look him in the eye. Stand tall, no
> matter what he's saying to you. He'll back down.
> You'll only have to do it once.

Epic fail. On all counts. Turns out, it's hard to look someone in the eye when their fist is in yours.

In the stained, cracked glass of the bathroom mirror my bruised face fits in nicely. It's time to go back. I've never missed a game of laser tag. Not in as long as I can remember. But I know I can't walk in there and face Ralph, not to mention Marc and friends.

Where do you go when what is sacred is ruined? You're supposed to get right back on the horse after a fall, they say. But I guess I'm not that kind of a guy. Not today.

When I'm sure the round has started, only then do I move. The bathroom door's familiar creak feels loud as a smack to the cheek, like a boot on the tile that just misses its mark.

I slide around the arcade, even though going through would be shorter. Good—Amanda's busy checking someone in with shoes and a lane. She doesn't see me walk, head down, toward the office, close the door, or fall onto the couch.

My ribs ache. My left ankle is doing a questionable thing. I don't understand. I don't see what I ever did. It's not a big deal to lose at laser tag. I used to lose all the time. I never beat anyone up over it.

The bruise on my cheek is not soothed by the line of salt water running over it. It tingles and stings but the feeling flows anyway. I sit at the computer and pull up my email. The existing draft looks cold and plain.

Delete.

My fingers spell out the first desperate thoughts that come to mind.

> Dad, where are you? Will you please write back,
> or call, or come visit? I need to know how to
> survive middle school. You must know, right?
> Because you did it?
>   I wish you were here. I don't understand why
> you have to be far away. There are times when I
> just really need you. This is one of those times.
> And it can't wait weeks, or however long until you
> write back. It's an emergency. I don't know what
> to do.

Footsteps approach the office door, and the knob turns. My impulse is to hide what I'm writing, to get it off the screen. I swiftly click.

Ralph steps into the office. "There you are," he says from behind me. "You okay?"

"Sure," I answer without turning from the computer. The email is gone. A small box in the corner reads *Message Sent.* Not *Draft Saved.* Not *Message Deleted.* Sent. I don't know what came over me. I don't know what came over me.

"I've never known you to miss a round," Ralph says. "What's going on, bud?"

"I have a lot of homework," I say.

"On a Friday?" Ralph asks. "Try again."

"I don't know." My fingers trace the edge of the keyboard, picking up a layer of dust. I want to say something true. "My stomach is a little upset. I was in the bathroom for a while and I missed the start, okay? Sorry."

"Ah," he says, with a deep chuckle. "Happens to the best of us. No need to be embarrassed. You coming in for round three?"

"I'm . . . afraid to." Also true.

"Alllll righty then," Ralph says. "You feel better, kid. It's just not the same in there without you."

7

FROZEN PEAS
AND FRIED CHICKEN

There's no hiding my face from Mom, of course. Waving to Ralph and Amanda from afar on the way out of the bowling alley is one thing, but a car ride and face-to-face dinner are in my immediate future.

"Hi, swee—Chester, what happened to your face?" Mom exclaims as I hop into the backseat.

"Just a little laser tag incident. I'm fine." I click my seat belt and turn toward the window.

Mom reaches back and grabs my chin. "That doesn't look fine. Why didn't Ralph or Amanda call me?" She turns off the ignition, as if to go inside. If she does, my cover is blown.

"Mom. Really. It's okay. Can we please just go home?"

"Look at you! They should have called."

"I didn't even tell them," I admit. "It was fast and I didn't want to make a big deal." That much is true.

"What happened?"

"Some kid was running in the arena, like you're not supposed to. He bumped me and I banged into the wall. No big deal. Things happen."

Mom sighs and starts the car. "Well, let's get you home."

Relief floods me. Relief, and an extra surge of hatred for Marc Ruff-road. He's supposed to be *my* problem. Not Mom's. I'm used to him knocking me around, but why'd he have to go and leave visible evidence?

Mom drags me into the bathroom for a closer look under the light. Yikes. The ring around my eye has swollen up considerably since it happened. She pokes my bruise.

"Ow."

"Is it sore?"

Duh, Mom.

"Have you been icing this?"

"No." That had not occurred to me.

"I'm gonna make you an ice pack."

Mom bustles away. She's in hard-core Mom mode, so there's no point in arguing.

Maybe the ice will help. But I could probably use something more than that, to take the edge off the throbbing.

The back of the Tylenol bottle explains everything. One pill, every four hours.

Mom's usually the one who administers medicine, but that would mean admitting how much my head is hurting, so I take the pill while she's still in the kitchen.

The bright overhead light makes my eye water, so I retreat to the soft lamplight of my bedroom. Better.

Mom swoops in with a small bag of frozen peas and a thin dish towel. She plops it on my face. Oh, it does feel kinda good. At least now I feel like an action movie hero, or something.

"Thanks."

"Keep it on for ten minutes. Then we'll have the peas with dinner," Mom says. Way to bring me down a notch.

"Okay."

She runs a hand through her hair. "Christopher will be here any minute. I need to freshen up."

"I'm fine, Mom. Do your stuff."

○-

While Mom's in the shower, I sneak out to the living room and peck into my email one-handed. I'm still embarrassed about sending such a desperate message, but maybe desperation will make Dad see how important his answer is to me. He could be on a mission, I know, but still.

Nothing. Inbox: zero.

When the blow dryer starts humming, I power down and go back to my room.

"That's good on the ice, honey," Mom says as she passes my door. "Come set the table."

Three place settings, three glasses of water, two beers, and a strawberry lemonade. I'm never allowed to drink pop, but once a week I get to have a sugary drink. All the best things happen on Fridays.

I touch my sore face. Well, usually.

We're almost ready when the knock comes. Mom rushes to wipe down the last bit of the countertop, then stares at her reflection in the microwave door and fluffs her hair.

"I'll get it," I offer. Her hair is going to look exactly the same one minute from now, but it makes her feel better to pretend it's different. The least I can do is buy her some time.

"Thanks, baby," she says, swirling up a tube of lip gloss.

I open the door. "Hi."

"Hey, Chester." Christopher holds up two plastic takeout bags. "Fried chicken too-night!" he bellows, in an extra-corny voice.

"Yum," I answer. All the best things.

We step into the light.

"Whoa, that's quite a shiner." Christopher drops the goofy tone. "You okay, pal?" He swoops in and I lock the door behind him.

"I'm good."

"Chester had a little accident at the bowling alley," Mom explains.

Mom has had one or two other boyfriends over the years. Mostly when I was really little. When Christopher came around it had been a while. He's nice enough.

Mom stands by the table looking pink of cheek and glossy of lip. Christopher scoops her into his arms. "Hey, beautiful," he says. "Happy to see me?"

"Happier to see that chicken," she says, eyeing the bucket over his shoulder.

Christopher groans into her neck. "You're killing me."

"I'm starving," she says. "And I love a man who keeps me in chicken." They laugh.

There are five things I like about Christopher.

Number one: He knows to pop the lid off the chicken bucket during the drive so the chicken doesn't steam itself soggy. We are men who prefer our chicken skin extra crispy.

"How was your day, Chester? Other than this situation." Christopher pantomimes a circle around his own eye as he settles into his usual dinner seat. "You wanna talk about it?"

"It was fine."

Mom swoops toward the kitchen, hefting the bags. "That's what he always says," Mom adds. She mimics my voice, making me sound flat and terrible. "'Fine.'"

Number two: Mom smiles a lot when he's here.

"'Fine' is fine," Christopher says. "Not as good as 'good,' but it'll do." He smiles at me. "You bowl today?"

He likes to know my scores. Sometimes I do really well. I've gotten good. "A little, but today was laser tag day."

"Right, right." He nods. "Do you know how lasers are made?"

Number three: He is smart. He knows interesting stories about important things.

"Not really," I say. "But it's not real lasers anyway."

Christopher laughs. "Yeah, no sense in lopping off body parts for fun. But 'concentrated infrared light beam tag' just doesn't have the same ring to it."

We smile.

Mom and Christopher hold hands off and on while we eat, which is pretty weird. They do this all the time. He's left-handed and she's right-handed, so when they're just using their forks it works okay. But it makes no sense to eat fried chicken this way. Obviously Mom was kidding when she said she was happier to see the chicken, but still. On the upside, holding hands slows them down, which means all the more chicken for me.

I chew steadily while they catch up about the past week. Mom tells stories about her annoying coworkers at the car rental office. Christopher has some kind of office job that I don't understand but it has a lot to do with "the market."

Number four on the list of things I like: He's not around all the time. He doesn't try to take over.

We mostly see Christopher on the weekends. He has a daughter who lives with him during the week. And Mom can't go out at night all that much, because of me, so here we are. They text a lot. A LOT. Mom sits on the couch most nights laughing into her phone. It works for us. While she's distracted I have more time to work on my spycraft. She doesn't even notice me printing out maps or researching encryption ciphers. Simply clearing the search history helps cover my tracks. It's probably not necessary. Mom might not even know the search history exists. But spies have to be thorough.

This weekend, I had planned to work on memorizing Morse code. But now, I'm not sure my eyes and head will be up for that kind of focus. My cheek and temple are throbbing despite the ice and Tylenol. I kinda just want to lie down.

My stomach, now full of chicken, starts to ache too. It's not the chicken's fault, but maybe I should have gone easier.

"Can I be excused?" I slide out of my chair without waiting for permission. "I'm going to my room."

"Mmm-hmm," Mom says, which means she isn't really listening. Christopher's hand on hers is what matters. Well, okay then. I have bigger things to deal with than boring romance anyway.

"Hey, Ches," Christopher calls after me. He does that sometimes, shorten my name like we're buds. He makes it work, I guess. "I brought a couple DVDs. Your pick."

Number five: He doesn't try to take Mom away and have her to himself, like all the others. He got me a bunch of sports stuff and on Saturdays sometimes we toss a ball around. It's not the highlight of my week, or anything, but it's not bad. Neither of us is really the sporty type, so it's pretty chill. Christopher says everyone should know the basics of ball handling, and I'm all for learning new skills. Spies have to be versatile.

"Take a look at the movie choices," he says. "If you don't like them, we can stream something." He doesn't expect me to hide in my room all night while they watch TV.

"In a little while," I say. "I want to work on my homework."

"Sure, sure," he says. "I'll catch up with your mom a bit."

"Whatever." I'm already in the hallway.

It turns out there are six things I like about Christopher.

Number six: I don't have a list of things I don't like about him.

8

SATURDAY WITH CHRISTOPHER

My face feels better in the morning, which is a relief. It doesn't necessarily look better, though. There's practically a whole rainbow of colors represented on my cheekbone.

My morning routine stays the same on the weekends, for simplicity. The difference is that Mom and Christopher won't come out of the bedroom until later, since no one has to go to school or work. That gives me plenty of time to check my email and read over Dad's past messages. I've written to him before about my problems with Marc Ruff-you-up, so looking over those old responses might help me until I hear back again.

Guys like him lash out from weakness. You are strong.

It's okay to focus on your homework. But is
there anyone in school that you'd like to try to be
friends with? There can be strength in numbers.

Dad's words remind me that he's out there somewhere,
caring about me. I hope he's safe.

The toilet flushes on the other side of the apartment.
They're up. I log out as Christopher pops out of the hallway,
headed for the kitchen.

He yawns. "Eggs? Bacon? Waffles? What's your pleasure?"

I had my routine cereal already, but one of the benefits of
Saturday is second breakfast. "Not sure we have any bacon," I
answer.

"Well then, how about a big pile of eggs and toast, then we
toss a ball around for a bit."

"Sure."

"Let's do it. You man the toaster?"

"It is my rightful domain."

Christopher hums while he scrambles up some eggs. I
set the table in between toast rounds. The eggs are ready in
a flash.

"Eggs a la Ro-Ro," Christopher says. The scrambled eggs
are extra fluffy, with cream cheese and tiny chunks of ham,
the way his daughter, Aurora, apparently likes them. The first
time he made them for us I was skeptical, but they're actually
super good.

I pile the last two slices on Mom's plate and glance down the hallway toward the bedrooms.

Christopher reads my mind. "Your mom wants to sleep in extra long today," he says.

I glance at the clock. "Even past nine?" That's rare.

"It was a long week. And a little guy time is always good, right?" He smiles.

Oh. I see what this is.

We sit down. The truth is, it's nice to have another guy around sometimes. The musky smell of his deodorant and his shaving soap is like woods in winter, very different from all the floral stuff Mom wears. Maybe the brands he uses are similar to Dad's. Maybe this is what it might feel like if Dad still lived here. Maybe we'd make eggs together and let Mom sleep in and play sports and watch movies. Or maybe it'd be totally different, but for sure I wouldn't have to wonder if he ever got punched in the face in sixth grade, or what advice he has for me. Because he'd be here, and I could just ask him.

It doesn't take us long to plow through a couple of scoops of eggs apiece. Christopher sits back and pats his mouth with a napkin. "What's your pleasure? Football? Basketball? A little tennis action?"

"To be honest," I say, "I don't know if I'm up for sports right now."

"Face hurts?" Christopher asks.

"Yeah."

He grabs our plates to clear. He's walking away when he says, "You wanna talk about what happened?"

The sink runs, the plates clatter. Christopher comes back to the doorway.

"Nothing happened."

There's a silence, a long awkward moment where the lie hangs out there. I don't know if he feels it too. If he guesses. What I do know is that Mom and Christopher don't keep secrets from each other. It's sweet and everything, but if I tell him the truth, she'll know all about it. And I can't have that.

"Well, I think we've exerted ourselves enough," Christopher says, patting his stomach. "What should we do instead? Care to just go for a drive?"

"Okay." It's simpler to agree than to explain why I need to stay home and sit by the computer all day. Something to take my mind off things probably wouldn't hurt either.

We end up at the best ice cream parlor in town, mere minutes after it opened for the day. Third breakfast? Excellent.

My favorite is a scoop of Superman in a waffle cone; Christopher chooses pralines and cream in a dish.

Observation: Christopher eats his ice cream with the

spoon upside down. I am not sure this has meaning, apart from enhancing ice-cream-to-tongue contact. But why not just get a cone then?

We lick in companionable silence. Turns out there's a number seven on the list of things I like about him: he doesn't have to be talking all the time.

"There's something I wanted to talk to you about," Christopher says, between bites.

Of course he would say that, two seconds after I add the observation to my list. "Okay." Please let it not be about who punched me in the face.

"You may have noticed that things are getting a little more serious between me and your mom."

Oh, this. Whew. "I think they got serious around the time you started spending the night," I say.

Christopher laughs. "Fair enough. That was definitely a level up. But what I'm saying is that we might begin spending even more time together. Not just our Friday nights."

"I'll be twelve in the summer," I tell him. "Then you can take her out on dates without getting a babysitter." Christopher has more money than we do, so paying for babysitters isn't really a problem. They choose to be home with me, which is actually kind of nice.

"How do you feel about me being around more? Or, maybe even you and your mom coming over to visit at my house sometimes? We haven't done that yet."

"It's fine." Do we really need to make a big deal about it?

Christopher licks his ice cream, spoon upside down. "That's it?"

"Mom likes having you around. You make her happy."

"She makes me happy too. But my question really is how YOU feel about it, Chester. Because it affects you too."

It really doesn't.

"Sometimes I sense that you might be having a hard time," Christopher says. "I don't want to do anything to add to that."

How does he sense that? It's supposed to be a secret. "I'm fine," I assure him. "We're fine."

"That's great." Christopher looks relieved, but still serious. "I just want you to know how important family is to me. It's been just me and Ro-Ro for a while now, and it's been just you and your mom. When a relationship gets serious, it can disrupt our sense of home and family. And that's a big deal."

I've seen enough movies to know what happens next in this situation. "Is this the part where I'm supposed to say, 'If you hurt her, I'm going to have to kill you'?" I am a spy-in-training, after all.

The corner of Christopher's mouth twitches. "Yes, of course. But let's hope it doesn't come to that."

"Definitely."

"Okay, well, thanks for letting me share those thoughts," he says. "I know it's not always easy for guys like us to talk about feelings. It would be natural for you to feel like I'm interrupting your family. But I really want you to feel comfortable with me and your mom being a couple."

I shrug. "You're not so bad, I guess."

Christopher grins. "Wow. High praise from Mister 'I'm Fine.'"

I can't help but smile too.

What I don't say is: *My family is already interrupted. But I'm putting us back together, one email at a time.*

9

THE MYSTERY ENVELOPE

Dad doesn't email me back all weekend. Not Saturday. Not Sunday. Not even by Monday before school.

My face is less puffy, but not totally back to normal. I'm dreading the questions that might come. I'm dreading facing Marc for the first time. Is this going to be the status quo from here on out, or will things go back to normal? Will he leave me alone? Do I need to tell Christopher that we need to add boxing to our sports rotation?

"Have a good day," Mom says, just as I'm contemplating coming down with something that means I'll have to stay home from school. But Mom can't afford to take days off from work. And I don't want her to worry. I'm fine. It'll be fine.

As the door swings open, an unfamiliar flutter near the outer doorknob startles me.

A bright red ribbon tied in a bow is looped over the handle, with something flat hanging from it the way an OPEN sign hangs on a shop door. The momentum of opening the door flipped it, so the ribbon is twisted in an X, as if the CLOSED side of the object was showing.

"Mom," I call. "Someone left someth—"

My voice trails off. The something is a small, stiff envelope. The paper is so nice that the corners are barely bendable. The flap side has a little raised logo from the fancy stationery shop at the mall. The smooth, perfect front has a little blue-and-gray boat with red sails in the top right corner and an ocean wave pattern along the bottom. It says CHESTER in neatly typed block letters.

It's for me?

"What, sweetie?" Mom says, stepping out of the kitchen.

"What is this?" I ask, turning my envelope over in my hands. *My* envelope.

"What is what?" She takes a sip of her coffee.

The rumble of the bus engine rounds the curve down the street. There's no time.

"Nothing. Have a good day, Mom." I close the door behind me. Just in case she's watching out the window, I carry the envelope by its ribbon in front of me, like an odd little purse. It's safe in my hands now.

Mom's voice was innocent—it seems clear that she didn't know what was waiting for me at the front door. She didn't use her fakey surprise voice. Anyway, it isn't really her style. There's only one person who would leave me such a mysterious note.

My heart swells. My mind races. The bus lumbers toward me. It's too late to get to the proper spot, so I rush straight to the end of my own entrance driveway.

The bus pulls up to where I stand and stops. Success!

The door glides open.

"Hi," I say, climbing aboard.

"Hi, Chester."

And that's it. The driver says nothing about the change in pickup location. The glow of my victory carries me like a wave, straight down the bus aisle to my usual seat. I tuck myself in as the bus lurches forward.

The note has to be from Dad. No other explanation makes sense.

My fingers fumble to find the gap between the flap and the pocket. *Scritch, scratch, scrape,* and the thing pops open.

Inside is a flat little card. It's decorated with the same boat and waves as the envelope, plus a cute little anchor. The typed message reads:

> Here's a puzzle for your pleasure,
>
> with an important prize at the end.
>
> Together, you can solve the mystery.
>
> You are not alone.

A puzzle? But how? Why? The back of the card is blank. Inside the envelope, there are two small blank notecards, folded in half. When I open the first card, it has a circled, handwritten 1 in the corner. The typed message says:

> Changes happen on the fly,   **1**
>
> Both must do their part and try.
>
> Do your best and don't ask why—
>
> Help will come out of the clear blue . . .

Weird. Extra super weird.

The second card has a circled 4 on it.

> **4**
>
>   full of joy
>
>   for your favorite toy.
>
>   some bragging rights,
>
>   name in lights.

None of this makes any sense. I have cards labeled 1 and 4. Was there supposed to be a 2 or a 3? Have I missed something? There's no way anything could have slipped out.

I check the seat around me just in case. Nothing.

What is Dad doing?

The bus pulls up to school and I realize I've gone the whole ride without giving a thought to Marc Ruff-houser. Maybe Dad knows what he's doing. Maybe he *did* get my email, and this is his way of saying he's here with me.

A puzzle, with a prize at the end. My heart leaps. Could it be?

LASAGNA WITH A SIDE
OF THE UNEXPECTED

Dad must be some kind of miracle worker, even from afar. Marc Ruff-landing is nowhere on my radar all morning—and believe me, my radar is tuned. The one class we had together—in other words, the reason he even knows I exist—ended after fall semester, so technically a Marc-free day is possible. Fingers crossed.

Lunchtime starts out as business as usual, though we share the same lunch period, so it's always a potential hot zone. I go through the line and always take the main course, no matter what it is. Today it happens to be lasagna, which is one of my favorites. It comes with a delicious, soft, buttery roll. On roll days, I splurge and pay the twenty-five cents extra for a second roll. If the world seems particularly cruel that day, I will even pony up fifty cents.

Today the world is complicated. Three rolls it is.

Marc and his friends sit in the center of the cafeteria. It is possible but difficult to not walk past his table. My route is circuitous, but I've tested various options and got it down to under a minute. My rolls are still warm.

My table is a small four-seater, far off in the corner, and I have it all to myself. I can read a book, or draw in my notebook, or work in my puzzle book, or hold up my fork and imagine Marc Ruff-rider behind bars where he belongs.

Best of all, it's one free hour when no one bothers me or even remembers I exist.

Usually.

Today is different.

I polish off the lasagna in short order. Midway through the second roll, my solitude is shattered.

"Chester?"

It must be my imagination. No one ever talks to me at lunch.

"Are you him?" A girl stands beside my table. She has lots of straight black hair with a perfect arc of bangs across her forehead. She's wearing a three-quarter-sleeve T-shirt with a bright rainbow design on the chest, and big mittens. Also a winter hat with a puff on top, and a thin scarf. It's very confusing.

"Pardon?"

She places her mittened hands on the lunch table. I cringe

slightly, because she didn't really look at the surface of the thing before she touched it. There's some kind of grime there, and now it's going to be ground into the yarn fibers of those mittens for all eternity.

"Are. You. Him?" she repeats, enunciating each word on a tiny puff of breath.

"I'm Chester," I tell her. "Who are you?"

"Chester Keene?"

"Yes."

"So you *are* him."

"Am who?"

She wrinkles her nose. "You're a little thick, aren't you?"

"I'm Chester Keene."

She sighs. "This conversation is going nowhere."

"What do you want?" No one comes looking for me. I don't really know what to say.

"I'm Skye. You're expecting me, right?" She plops down in the seat beside me and strips off the tainted mittens. The way she pulls them, the insides end up on the outside. And then she tosses them right onto the table! Now they are grimy inside and out.

I fight my gag reflex. "Are you sure you want to do that?"

Skye looks at me like I have two heads. "This is not going to be an easy assignment, is it?"

I pick up her mitten balls one by one and straighten them out for her.

She's still here.

"Can I help you with something?" Please say no. Please say no. Please say no.

"Yes, actually." *Dang.* "You're the one I'm looking for."

She pulls something out of her pocket. My whole body perks up, against my will. She tosses the item closer to me. "This is you, I guess."

The card has been folded, unfolded, and dented a fair bit. But the typed message is legible:

```
Among your classmates, not a Arthur,
    Quick to understand or function
   Together you will go much farther
Your fates are bound, an auspicious junction.
```

"So, you have the next clue, right? For our puzzle?"

Our puzzle? Dad's clue note floats back to me. *Help will come out of the clear blue . . .* Skye?

"I figured it out," Skye says. "You're Chester Keene. And we're supposed to work together."

Her card matches the two in my pocket. The type is the same and everything. It has been folded in the same neat way that suggests extreme care, because folding a notecard too casually results in one big mess of a crease.

"I don't know what you're talking about."

Skye sighs. "He said you might be difficult."

"Who said?" My pulse quickens.

"You know who." She points at her clue card. "*Not a Arthur* means not Chester A. Arthur, the twenty-first US president. And the dictionary definition of *keen* is 'quick to understand or function.'" She raises a brow at me. "Although . . ."

"Ha. Ha." I lift the clue card from her hand and study it. "*Arthur* and *farther* is not a great rhyme."

"Oh, give him a break," she says. "Don't you think this is cool?"

Skye has my full attention now. "Him?"

Skye gives me side eye.

The warm roll in my hand is as good to look at as anything. "I don't know what you're talking about." Is this a test?

I mean, Dad had said "work together."

"So, you don't have a clue for me?" she says. "Like this one?" She tosses a second card on the table. It's folded perfectly too, with a small circled 3 on the outside. It's all I can do not to pick it up and peek at the message.

"No." The resistance is automatic. But I have to overcome it. Dad's counting on me. "I mean, maybe."

"Hmph," Skye says. "Yes, you do. We should meet after school and work on this. Aren't you excited?"

"I go to the bowling alley after school," I tell her.

"Well, obviously today is different."

"I can't just change plans like that."

"Why not?"

"People are expecting me." That seems like an important thing to tell someone who might secretly be out to get you.

"So? Just tell them."

"My mom says I'm very schedule-oriented," I mumble.

"What does that mean?" Skye asks.

"It means, I like things to go a certain way. The way they always go."

"Your life must be so thrilling," she says, tapping her foot.

"It's an action-packed adventure."

She rolls her eyes at me. In books, people always talk about other people rolling their eyes. I never totally understood that before now.

"Do that again," I say.

"Do what?"

"Roll your eyes."

She does, but I'm not sure if it's to please me, or if she's still annoyed and just can't help it.

I smile. "I always pictured it differently," I tell her, as if she's going to care.

"Pictured what?"

"Rolling your eyes."

"You pictured me rolling my eyes?"

"Not you. Just . . . anyone."

She looks at me like I'm from outer space. I wish I was.

"Never mind," I tell her. "I'm weird."

"No kidding." Skye sighs. "So, I guess we go to the bowling alley," she says. "How do you get there?"

"I ride the bus."

"Which bus?"

"Number 223."

"Okay, then," Skye says. "I'll meet you on the bus. Bring your clue." She scoops up her cards and her mittens and drifts away. Over her shoulder floats, "Catch you later, Chester Keene."

UNDEFEATED

Skye stands with her hands on her hips in the middle of the bowling alley parking lot. Her big blue jacket flows behind her like a cape. The BOWL sign is on the blink. "So, this is where you hang out?"

"I guess."

The building does look a little shabby, even compared to the E-Z Check Cashing place next door. And that is a pretty low bar.

I hold the door open for Skye to enter. We blink, adjusting to the lack of sunshine.

"It's . . . nice." Her voice is full of false optimism. Like Mom saying "Dinner's ready" in a tone that lets me know everything came out a little bit burned.

I suppose I get where she's coming from. Looking at the

place with fresh eyes is not great for the self-esteem. The carpet is dingy and stained. The air smells like fried cheese and beer and lane wax. And also like feet. All the retro posters, neon signs, and dancing lights look super awkward in the afternoon.

"Hey, kiddo." Amanda's behind the counter already, spraying down some rental shoes. She tries to play it casual but she's checking us out hard-core. "Who's your friend?"

"This is Skye. Skye, this is Amanda. She owns the bowling alley."

"Hi." Skye gives a cheerful little wave. "Nice to meet you."

Amanda's smile is waaaay too chill. I'm suspicious. "Want me to set up a lane for you two?"

I glance at Skye. "Well, we have some work to do, actually."

"School project?"

"Not exactly," says Skye. "But the details would bore you." Luckily I had the forethought to warn her not to mention any puzzle-related activities to Amanda.

Amanda flicks some switches and the lights over Lane 6 come on.

"We should probably go to the office," I say, gazing meaningfully at Skye. "For some privacy."

"Nah. Come on," Skye says. "We might as well bowl while we work on it."

So we grab bowling shoes and troop over to Lane 6. Amanda keeps a special pair for me that no one else's feet have been in. They have Cs painted on the back instead of numbers.

The alley is more crowded than usual for a Monday after school. Which is to say, there are actually other people here.

There's a group already bowling in Lanes 1 and 2. Two men and two women. They glance at us, then they go about their business as if we don't exist. The way grown-ups always do.

It's weird that Amanda put them in Lanes 1 and 2, all the way down at the end like this. Usually she starts people in the middle, around Lane 10 or 12. The only time people bowl in Lane 1 or 24 is if the place is extra crowded, or it's a kid's birthday party and we have to roll out the bumpers. Well, some grown-ups like 23–24 because it's close to the bar, I guess. Lanes 1–2 are close to nothing except the restrooms and the emergency exit, which has a sign that it's alarmed but it really isn't.

Lane 6 is my personal favorite. My lucky number and all.

We dump our backpacks on the seats. I fold my green fleece vest carefully and lay it over my bag. Skye sheds her jacket in a heap. It's bright blue, too big for her, and made of a material that's slick and rich. The back says ALI 24–0 in letters that are kinda like sports jersey letters.

"What's that mean?" I ask. It's the kind of garment that's hard to look away from.

Skye holds up the jacket proudly. Under the writing there

are two large golden boxing gloves. "It's my mom's. Custom-made. She lets me wear it sometimes. She's a big fan."

"Of what?"

"Laila Ali!" Skye shrieks. Apparently this should be obvious.

"Who?" It always makes me nervous to ask. There are a lot of things other kids know that I don't know, especially about celebrities and stuff.

"She's a famous boxer. She fought twenty-four bouts and was undefeated. The greatest!" Skye mugs with her fists like a boxer. "Her dad was a famous boxer too."

Undefeated. Famous boxer. "Muhammad Ali?"

"Yeah!" Skye swirls away toward the ball rack, still mugging. "His record wasn't as perfect, but he was definitely amazing. The apple doesn't fall far from the tree and all."

"Do you know how to box? For real?" The footwork she's doing right now looks pretty good to me.

"A little," she says. "Mom has shown me some moves." Maybe Skye's the one I should be asking about boxing tips. Is that why Dad sent her to me? Things are starting to make sense.

"Do you think . . . I mean, maybe . . . can you teach me?" It would be good to be prepared, right? Just in case. If I knew how to fight back against a punch, maybe I wouldn't have ended up on the floor in a matter of seconds.

"Sure," Skye says. She hops once and lands with her feet

60

in a different position, fists up. "Basic fighting stance. Now you try."

I pull my fists up in front of my shoulders.

"No. Come over here. Stand next to me," Skye says. We step away from the chairs, up onto the smooth wooden approach area in front of the lane. Skye leads me into the stance, one move at a time. "Slide your right leg back at an angle. Keep your left foot pointed forward." She bounces. "This keeps you mobile. Bob and weave."

Bob and weave. Skye looks nimble. Next to her I feel like a blob.

"Elbows bent and tucked in by your waist." She flaps her arms wildly for a moment. "No chicken wings."

I mimic her.

"Thumbs always in front of your knuckles. Never tucked inside."

I pop them out.

"And alternate. Pow. Pow. Pow." She does a smooth, rhythmic move with her fists, keeping one low by her hip while the other punches forward, and then switching them.

My attempt is nowhere near as smooth, but as my fist jabs the air, it's not so hard to imagine it striking a target.

Skye stops punching after a short while. "See? You're getting the hang of it. And now, we bowl!" She hops down off the approach area and dips her fingers into the holes of several balls, patting them, rolling them, looking for a good fit.

The jacket that represents no defeats is piled in a heap on the floor, which bothers me. "Can I touch it?" I ask, reaching for the jacket. At the very least, it should be on a chair.

"Sure," Skye says.

Ooooh. The jacket feels smooth and cool and buttery. "It's nice." Actually, it's excellent. It folds nicely, and in a second I'll drape it over the chair, but for now I don't want to let it go.

There's something about it. I don't know why. It makes me feel like anything is possible. Laila Ali followed in her dad's footsteps, and she was undefeated.

12

BLUEBELL AND BUBBLE GUM

"I want this blue ball," Skye announces. She tries to pick it up, but her fingers swim in the holes and then they slip back out. "Ooof!" The ball thumps back onto the metal tray.

The other balls in our lane are all too heavy, too.

"There's a six-pound blue one somewhere," I tell her. "We'll just have to find it." Personally, I'm fond of the six-pound pink one. It looks like bubble gum, which I don't even like the taste of, but looking at it makes me happy for some reason.

Skye and I go to the ball storage racks at the back of the lanes. Behind us a ball goes *thump-sliiiiiiiiide-crash!* The grown-ups cheer. I can't help but look. She got a strike!

"Nice one, Lady," says one of the guys.

Lady does a little victory dance. Her big blond hair barely moves as the rest of her shimmies. "I'm gonna get you yet, Slim," she answers, pointing a finger at the guy.

How in the world does she bowl with nails that long? They're tiger-striped, and they curve at the ends.

"Nah. I'm just warming up." Slim cracks his knuckles.

"Slim?" Skye whispers to me.

I shrug. Slim's what my mom would call "stocky." We move down the row, in search of the lighter balls.

"Opposite nicknames are kinda cliché, don't you think?" Skye says, when we're out of earshot.

"I've never given it much thought," I answer, which is true.

Thump-sliiiiiiiide-crash! Slim left one pin standing. Lady howls with laughter.

"There's always a chubby guy called Slim," Skye explains. "It's so old-fashioned. I mean, that's like me calling you . . . Messy."

Yuck. "Who would do that? That's a terrible nickname."

"Hey, Mess," she says.

My face wrinkles. I can't help it.

Skye cracks up. "See?"

"Never do that," I tell her.

"I was just MESSing with you," she declares.

I snort. Then cough, trying to hold back the laugh that made me snort in the first place.

Skye laughs harder. "Did you just snort?"

I deploy my best innocent undercover spy expression. "I can neither confirm nor deny."

"You can admit it to me. We're on the same team." Skye puts her face near mine. "You think I'm funny."

I hope she's not incubating any hideous germs. My system is very sensitive. "I think you're the MESS," I answer.

Skye grins. She has this kind of smile that dares you not to smile back. "Now you're coming around."

And then her face is not near my face anymore, which is a relief, and she's grabbing a blue ball. "Aha!" She holds it aloft in triumph. The six-pounder.

When she brings it down, she lowers it to her mouth and kisses it right on the 6.

Ewww. "Gross," I tell her. "You don't know where that has been."

Skye ignores me. She whispers into its finger holes. "I shall call you Bluebell and you shall lead me to victory."

"You're celebrating too soon," I assure her. "I am a very good bowler."

"Everyone's a good bowler," she says.

This is categorically untrue. "Um," I mutter as we return to Lane 6.

"Listen," Skye says. "Some people make it all about knocking the pins down, but I prefer to bowl with style."

Knocking the pins down is the whole game. But Skye is the sort of person with whom you can't argue logic.

"Bowl with style?"

"Yeah. You have to be creative. And then the other person judges your style. Watch." She grabs Bluebell. "Are you watching?"

"Yeah."

Skye raises the ball above her head, does a little shuffle with her feet. Then she holds the ball to her left and does the foot thing again. Then she holds the ball to her right. The little dance move draws her forward every time. Up, shuffle. Left, shuffle. Right, shuffle. When she gets to the line, she moves the ball in a circle and then pushes it out from her chest like the worst-imaginable basketball toss a person has ever done in gym class. I have to compare it to basketball because there is no comparison to bowling whatsoever.

The ball thumps to the lane like a lead weight. It rolls center-ish until about halfway down the lane, then gives up and slides toward the gutter. Meanwhile Skye is still doing a punching thing with her arms. Up. Left. Right. Circle.

She backs up toward me. "So? How'd I do?"

The electronic scorecard on the monitor over our heads registers zero.

"You didn't hit anything."

Skye puts her hands on her hips. "You're supposed to judge my delivery style. Rate me."

"Oh. Um. Nine?"

"Nine?" she echoes. "Really?" She pauses. "It's a scale of one hundred, just so you know."

"Oh." Naturally. "So . . . ninety?"

Skye grins. "You're going easy on me. I'm just warming up."

Bluebell thumps and whooshes out of the ball return. It knocks noses with my pink ball. I run my hand over its familiar smooth surface. Amid the whirlwind that is Skye, a quiet moment with my ball feels refreshing. This, I understand. This, I know how to do. Sliding my fingers into the holes is like coming home.

"What's its name? Your ball."

Uh. "Bubble Gum?" I hug it to my chest in all its pinkness. "We go way back."

Skye nods sagely. To Bubble Gum she says, "Pleasure."

I focus on my form and deliver my shot. *Thump-sliiiiiiiiide-crash!* Eight of the pins fall down.

TEAMWORK, WHAT A CONCEPT

"Ten," Skye announces. "You didn't do anything interesting."

"Knocking down eight pins is interesting to me."

Skye nods. "That's why I gave you points at all. That, and the leg thing." She imitates my bowling form in ridiculous fashion. Like a rogue curtsy. I laugh out loud.

My eight rolls up on the screen overhead, but of course it scores itself as Skye's second shot. I don't like this one bit.

"We should get a paper scorecard from Amanda. There's still a pad of them behind the desk." There's a group of old-timers who come in occasionally. They like to score with pencil. It reminds me too much of math homework, but some of them can't see the small print on the electronic screen so well. Amanda's good at taking care of people that way.

I start walking away from the lane, just as Bubble Gum whooshes out of the ball return.

"Who needs a scorecard?" Skye taps her temple. "I'm already a winner in here."

"We're supposed to be working on our cipher," I remind her. "Our puzzle."

"Let's look at the clues," Skye agrees.

We bring out the cards.

"Part of mine makes more sense now," she says. "*Amanda's place* must be the bowling alley."

I glance toward the desk. Amanda's still watching us with interest. I flick my hand at her and she turns away, acting all innocent, like she hasn't just been spying. I've never had a friend over before, ever, but that's no reason to stare.

"Usually the important words are the clues," Skye says, pointing to her own card. "*Grasping. Claw. Blinking.* It's weird that it's capital *B* and *K*."

```
Amanda's place is
Like grasping
Claw your way to
A flashing BlinKing
```

"Let me see yours again," Skye says. We trade. She studies my card while I find myself staring in the direction of the arcade.

```
                              full of joy
                  for your favorite toy.
                  some bragging rights,
                      name in lights.
```

"I don't know," she says. "Yours is less interesting. *Favorite. Bragging. Name in lights.* And nothing is capitalized."

"Not even the beginning of the lines," I point out. It has been driving me nuts.

"Wait." Skye turns my note sideways and folds it in half, with the writing showing. Smashes it in half, more like. "Fold it like this," she says.

I fold her half neatly. Skye grabs it from me and pushes the two cards together.

```
         Amanda's place is full of joy
      Like grasping for your favorite toy.
      Claw your way to some bragging rights,
       A flashing BlinKing name in lights.
```

"Now, that's a proper clue." Skye waggles her eyebrows at me.

"And I think I know what it means," I tell her. "Follow me."

"Oooh." Skye leaps up and does a little dance. I'd give it 75 out of 100.

We scoot around the ball return, toward Lanes 3–4. In Lanes 1–2, the grown-ups are six frames into their game.

"It's three fifty-five," says the wiry guy. "I need a cigarette."

"All right, Ice, let's go," says Lady, reaching for her purse. "Sugar, you coming?"

The other woman says, "Shoulda gone out five minutes ago." Sugar's voice is hoarse, exactly like you'd expect from someone who probably smokes a lot. She stands up too. She's shorter than all the others.

"I'll hold down the fort," Slim says, settling deeper into his seat.

The others troop toward the emergency exit. I narrow my eyes at them. *Rule breakers*. Somehow they've figured out that it isn't really alarmed.

"Where are we going?" Skye's voice is excited.

"You'll see." We approach the arcade. When we get to the claw machine, I raise my hands with a flourish, like Vanna White. "Behold."

Skye beholds. "Bling King!" She claps her hands in joy. The sign at the top of the claw machine is indeed flashing and blinking its name in lights.

"So, this is probably it, right?"

"Absolutely. I love a play on words." Skye embraces the huge machine, throwing out her arms and pressing her cheek against the grimy glass. Yuck.

"You are so strange," I tell her.

Skye grins. "But my methods are effective." She pulls out of the hug, and there's another folded notecard in her hand. "This was taped to the side of the glass."

BEATING THE BLING KING

Skye opens the new card and we look at it together:

> One of these things is not like the others.
>
> One of these things uses lightning to drive.
>
> One of these things is not like the others.
>
> One of these things holds the key to the hive.

"One of these things is not like the others?" Skye reads aloud.

"One of the toys?" I suggest. We peer through the glass. A fantastical menagerie of stuffed animals stares back at us. They are small and medium, all similarly plush. Pandas, teddies, killer whales, giraffes, eagles, several species of dinosaur rendered in varying degrees of realism. I wink at Old Brown

Eyes, the fluffy-winged owl that I typically aim for. He's been in here for years, the same exact guy. I've caught him dozens of times. No one else has. Most of the other animals turn over from time to time. It's just me and Old Brown Eyes. I feel like he appreciates me. If he ever gets chosen for real, I'll miss him.

"What about the most interesting words?" Skye says.

"*Lightning, drive, key, hive*?"

"*Key* rhymes with *bee*." Skye presses close to the glass again. "Is there a bee?"

"There, in the back." I point. A medium honeybee with a round black-and-yellow-striped body and jaunty white wings.

"That must be it."

"How is it different from the others?" I ask. "I mean, it's the only bee, but there's only one of several other things too. A bee doesn't require lightning to drive."

"I don't know," she says. "Maybe the clue is on it, or inside it. Let's get the bee!" Skye grabs the joysticks. "How the heck do you work this thing?"

"You have to put coins in first. Amanda has them."

We troop over to the desk. Amanda gives us each a handful of quarters. You'd think we were circus performers, the way she's gawking at us. Sheesh.

"If you need more, you know where to find me," she says.

Amanda gives me unlimited quarters for the games. The only downside is that I have to put back my winnings, and I can't play if a paying customer wants to use the machine. It works out fine for me. Amanda says impeccable arcade skills are a good thing to have in my back pocket. Someday I will win a lot of bets, she says. But I can't really picture myself becoming a crane-machine grifter.

Skye pops two quarters into the Bling King. She grips the joysticks and places her feet in a fighting stance. Her face turns fierce. "Let's do this thing."

Uh-oh. Skye does not know how to do this thing. She wiggles the joysticks left and right, up and down, watching the claw slide its way along the ceiling. Her moves are too big and rushed. The claw jolts rapidly from glass wall to glass wall.

"Gently," I say.

She flexes her fingers and tries again. She eventually gets it sort of positioned over the bee.

"Aha!" Skye drops the claw. It's totally not going to work, but I don't know how to tell her. Her smile is huge.

The claw grazes the bee's wing, then closes around air.

"Boo," she says, tugging the joysticks. "Hey, it's not moving anymore!"

"You have to pay again now," I tell her.

Skye gapes at me. "Whoa. That's a racket."

I shrug.

Skye steps back. "Okay, your turn."

"Oh, no, you can try again." I pump in two quarters for her. It seems like she's having fun.

Skye resumes her fighting stance. *Take notes, Keene.* "Cool. Thanks." She's still moving the joysticks a little too hard.

"Gently," I say. "You want to get it farther back than last time. The claw has to hug the whole bee, not just the wings."

"Hug the bee," she murmurs, concentrating fiercely. "Hug the bee."

"Aaaaand . . . now!" I tell her.

She drops the claw. It hugs the bee. Sort of. The machine is built to trick you.

"Yesssss!" Skye celebrates too early. The bee begins to fly, but it still has to be carried all the way over to the drop hole. It slips out halfway there. "Oh, shucks," Skye laments.

"Maybe not," I suggest. "Maybe that's exactly what was supposed to happen. Look."

I point toward where the bee used to be. Poking up from the sea of stuffed animals is a plastic package with an action figure inside.

One of these things is not like the others.

"Oooh." Skye cups her hands against the glass and peers through them like imaginary binoculars. "Is that the Flash?"

"Yeah. See the lightning bolt on his ear?" I'm not a comic book expert, but I know my way around the obvious.

Skye glances at me. "I know what the Flash looks like," she says. "It was rhetorical."

Oh. I stare through the glass alongside her. My mind is

back on the puzzle at hand. "Did you know that another word for *lightning drive* is *flash drive*?"

"Most people say *flash drive*," Skye says.

Maybe she thinks I'm being rhetorical. "I mean, our clue is about lightning. And how . . ."

". . . one of these things is not like the other." Skye finishes my thought. She crosses her arms. "The Flash is different."

"The Flash is way better than a bee."

"Not universally," Skye argues. "I thought the Wasp was pretty awesome. Didn't you see *Ant-Man and the Wasp*?"

"The Wasp and the Flash would be on the same team."

"Maybe," she says. "Depends on the fight."

I don't really know how to argue with that. "Why does he have to make this so difficult?" I ask.

"Because it's more fun," she says. "If it was too easy it'd be boring."

"Boring?" I say. "Serving the government and saving lives?"

Skye rolls her eyes. Apparently she loves to do that. "Your turn."

"You can go again," I offer. "You're just getting the hang of it."

Skye smiles. "Okay." Of course, getting the claw to grip a plastic package is even harder than going for the bee. Her first attempt goes quite awry.

"Your turn," she says.

"I'll try when you're tired of trying," I say.

"We should take turns," she says. "That's what's fair."

"I'll go if you haven't got it when we're down to four quarters." Two would probably be enough, but I believe in insurance.

Skye cocks an eyebrow. "Someone's confident."

"I basically live here," I remind her with a shrug. "I'm pretty good at all the games."

"Okay, hot stuff." She steps back and crosses her arms. "Show me what you got."

"Okay." My hands are sweating a bit as I approach the joysticks. I wasn't trying to brag. I just didn't want to take the fun out of it for her. But now I'm on the spot. My elbows feel like jelly.

The Flash raises his brow at me, as if to say *You're the little punk who's coming for me?*

I look him in the eye. "Yeah, I'm coming for you."

THE FLASH

Skye is impressed by my Bling King mastery. I move the joystick like I'm doing laser surgery. Right to the spot, down and up, with the claw hooked exactly around the lipped corner of the plastic package. The Flash rises like Superman. Or, like the Wasp, I suppose. If that's how you roll. I glide him to the drop hole.

One and done. I couldn't have asked for a more perfect run. My palms are too slick to reach through the trapdoor right away. Gotta dry them on my jeans.

"Wow." Skye smiles at me like I've cracked a code that will save all humanity or invented the cure for a horrible and deadly disease. I feel like a winner. It's a good feeling. A warm flood through my whole self. I don't want it to end.

It's a little hard to get the Flash out through the flap. I work on it while Skye returns the excess quarters to Amanda.

"Here we go." I hold him up in triumph when she gets back.

We troop back to Lane 6 with our prize. The adults in Lanes 1–2 are still only halfway through their second game. It looks like they haven't bowled a single frame since they went for their smoke break. They're all hanging around in the chairs vaguely chatting.

As we walk by, Slim says, "We need to take Fido out."

"Nah, he's fine," says the wiry man.

"Ice is right," Lady agrees. "Less damage, less drama."

"It's all about the van," says the other woman. "We keep Fido tied up and he can't hurt anything."

"Who names their dog Fido anymore?" Skye whispers. We plant ourselves in the chairs of our lane, just like the grown-ups. I guess today's the day for not bowling.

The Flash, of course, is encased in molded plastic. The front piece is welded to the back piece by four round buttons at the corners. I can fit my fingers into the slit between, but no matter how much I pull, the halves will never separate. I already know this, and yet I always try. Every time. I have no idea why.

Skye takes the Flash in her hands and regards him very seriously. "You must first escape your packaging, and thus prove you are worthy."

The laugh bubbles up in my throat against my will. I can't stop it. And . . . I find . . . I don't want to. "You're a nut."

Skye raises her chin. "Nuts are a staple food in many cultures. They have been since caveman times. Have some respect."

"I know where there are scissors." I hop up to go get them.

We cut open the package and the diminutive hero pops out into our hands. Between the layers of the thin folded piece of cardboard that announces his name, there is a note card marked 6.

Skye picks up the Flash packaging. "How did he do that, I wonder?"

"Do what?"

"Open this box and then reseal it to look new."

"Spies have all kinds of skills," I answer. That's the best thing to say when the real answer is, I have no idea.

Skye tilts her head and gives me a funny look.

"I mean, you never know what a mission will entail, right? Sometimes they have to improvise."

"Spies . . ." Skye taps her lips and narrows her eyes. That's when it hits me. What I've just said. What I've just revealed.

My cheeks burn with shame and horror. *Oh, no. Oh, gosh.* "Um, no, I mean . . . uh . . ." Quick! Say something. Anything. Explain. Make a joke. But my brain is frozen. "I—um . . ."

How could I be so careless? Did I just totally blow Dad's cover? I was feeling so good, so comfortable, working the clues with Skye. But I shouldn't have assumed that just because Dad sent her to me, that she knew.

Start again. "Forget it. I didn't mean—"

"Shhh!" Skye says, glancing furtively from left to right.

"We don't know who might be listening." She lowers her voice. "May I speak freely?"

"Of course." My face is still hot with embarrassment. I let my guard down for a minute, but it won't happen again. All I can do is hope I didn't mess things up for Dad.

Skye leans in. "My dad *has* been acting a little strange lately. Spending time with some mysterious people. And now, these cryptic clues? Something has to be up, right?"

"Totally," I agree. Skye's dad must be a spy too. "They brought us together for a reason."

"Yes," Skye says. "And we're gonna solve this thing. And show them we're ready for anything."

"If they need our help, things must be pretty serious."

"As serious as it gets," Skye agrees. "But I like you, Chester Keene. It's gonna work out just fine."

She's awfully confident, considering we don't really know what we're up against here. I'm not sure what to say. "So, should we get on with it?"

"Our secret spy mission?" Skye winks. "Yes, and we already have our next clue!" She unfolds the notecard that was tucked behind the Flash.

> Your next treasure waits in a honeyed box
>
> With a trio of bears and golden locks.
>
> Something borrowed, something blue,
>
> a lucky lane and the number two.

We read it out loud. Twice. The clue makes no more sense the second time. "What do you think it means?"

Skye shrugs. "We should bowl while we think about it."

The rest of the afternoon blinks by in an instant. We "fancy bowl," as Skye calls it, until it's time to get picked up. We've been talking through possibilities—the blue pack of Teddy Grahams in the vending machine seemed promising, at first—but we haven't solved the puzzle and we're running out of time.

"My mom will be here soon," I tell Skye at the end of a tenth frame. "She gets off work at five and she picks me up at five-thirty."

"I have to go anyway. I'm meeting my dad at the Road-house," Skye says.

What? My heart does a funny flutter. "You're meeting your dad? Now?"

"Yeah, of course." Skye slides out of her bowling shoes and into her regular shoes.

"But, then, can't you just ask him what's going on with these clues?"

"Oh, no." Skye grins. "We can't openly discuss spy business. Duh."

Of course. That makes sense. "The Roadhouse diner in the mall?"

"Yup." Skye hooks her fingers into the bowling shoes. "It's a known spy hangout." She winks at me. "Don't go telling on us."

"I would never." It's hard to tamp down my excitement. A known spy hangout? Right in our very own mall? Does my dad go there too? My mind clicks around this new information. Round and round and round it, thinking hard. *Known spy hangout.* It fills my head. There's no extra space to process the fact that Skye is busy stacking up all the clue cards and dropping them in her bag. It happens right in front of me, and somehow I say nothing.

"I believe you." Skye shoulders her backpack. "You're obviously very trustworthy. See you at school?"

"Sure," I answer. "See you at school."

Skye waves to Amanda as she walks out the door, carrying all the clues with her.

16

PLANET EARTH

When Mom rolls up five minutes late, I'm sitting on the curb in front of the bowling alley waiting for her. Five minutes is a long time. Much too long, on a day like this, to be left alone with my thoughts with no distraction. It's all I can do to hold my knees and breathe.

Skye took all the clues, leaving me nothing to hold, to touch, to study, to remind myself that what's happening is all real. Dad has reached out. Dad needs my help. Dad has sent me this . . . person . . . to work with, because whatever is going on is too big for him and me alone.

What does it mean?

I've dreamed of the day Dad might be actually physically here. But to know that he was so close, close enough to hang a note on our doorknob, and I still can't see him? It hurts. And I'm scared of what it means. What kind of trouble could he be in that prevents him from just knocking on the door?

The worst thought is that whatever trouble he's in might be my fault. He's here because he's answering my desperate plea to see him, my cry into the void for him to help me. Did I put him at risk? Did his coming here somehow reveal him to his enemies?

Mom rolls down the passenger window. "Offer you a lift, good sir?"

It takes me a moment to shake off the flood of thoughts assaulting my brain. *Mom is here. Stand up. Get in the car.*

"And how, old chap." I slip into the backseat and buckle in.

"How are things, today, sir?" Mom asks.

I make my voice very formal. "It's been a day, James." Boy howdy.

"Where to, Mr. Keene?" Chauffeur Mom (aka James) says. This is a game we play.

It occurs to me to ask if we can eat at the diner too. But we probably can't afford it. Mom works hard and we do okay, but we don't have a lot of extra.

"Home, James." It's the answer Mom's expecting. For the game. She's already pulling out of the parking lot in that direction.

"Very good, sir."

When we get home, I put my things in my room. It feels

stuffy in here. As if the air is full of dust. When was the last time we vacuumed this place, anyway?

We keep the vacuum in the cleaning supplies cabinet. It doesn't take that long to do the whole apartment. It's not that big. If I plug into a certain spot, I can do the whole place without unplugging once. It's a science. My hands know how to wrap and unwrap the cord from the base as I sweep my way from corner to corner. There's magic in the rhythm of it.

"Dinner," Mom says, when I finally shut the vacuum off.

She's already set the table. The food is waiting. One of my favorite meals: meatloaf, potatoes, and green beans. Well, green beans are not exactly a favorite, but they are the least-objectionable vegetable.

We eat quietly. When we're done, Mom starts to clear the plates, which is my job.

"I'll do it."

She lets me take the plates from her. Mom packs up the leftovers while I wash the dishes. The running water feels clean and good on my hands. I wash everything: plates, cups, pans, silverware, prep bowls, even the empty green bean can. The countertop, the faucets, the stovetop, the sink. I scrub until everything glistens.

When there's nothing left to clean, I come out. Mom's sitting on the couch with her feet tucked up under her. She cups a mug of tea in her hands. One more mug to wash. When did she make herself tea?

"What's the matter, sweetie?" Mom asks.

"Nothing."

"You're cleaning like you're upset."

I want things to look neat and orderly. I want things to make sense. "I'm not upset," I lie.

Without Dad's notecards in my pocket, everything feels out of control. Every breath stretches my chest too much. My body might soon fill with air and float away. Those messages from Dad are what hold me to the ground. But no email has come. The clues have left me in limbo.

"Will you come sit with me?" Mom pats the cushion next to her.

If I run away now, she'll worry even more. Anyway, I'm not opposed to an occasional snuggle. It feels nice. Mom puts her arm around me and scrunches me up next to her. She nuzzles my head and sighs into my hair. "Oh, my sweet boy."

"Don't get mushy!"

"But I love you so MUSH." Mom plunges her face into my neck and actually zerberts me. Like I'm five.

"Gross," I declare, even though her weirdness makes me laugh. She squeezes me and I let her.

"What should we watch?" she asks. "*Planet Earth*?"

"Yeah, an ocean episode," I suggest. We like *Planet Earth*.

It's very soothing. It's very pretty. The animals are part of an elaborate system and totally free at the same time. It's fascinating.

Mom pushes buttons on the remote. She gets the show all cued up, then pauses. "Is there anything you want to talk about first?"

"No."

"You sure?"

"I'm sure." I haven't actually done any of my homework, for the first time in my entire life. That might be of interest. But Mom's side is warm and her arm is solid and tight around me. I might not float away after all.

17

NUMBER TWO

Tuesday morning is rather stressful, but not nearly as much as I expected. I finish one homework assignment on the bus ride to school, and another during homeroom. The rest of my teachers believe me when I tell them I wasn't feeling well last night. They all say it's okay. I always do all my homework, so I guess they believe me. And it's kind of true anyway.

Lunch today is sloppy joes. They're better than you'd think. Some people complain about school lunch, no matter what is served. As for me, the only thing I really hate is chipped beef on toast. Yuck.

I wind my way through the cafeteria. Marc Ruff-draft crows loudly about something that makes everyone at his table laugh. He's too far away to notice me, but somehow it's impossible not to notice him.

"Chester, Chester, bo-bester." Skye's singsong voice dances behind me. My safe route has been infiltrated.

She's seated at a table full of girls from her class. Seventh graders. They chatter loudly, talking all over and against each other. They appear to be debating the relative merits of different writing implements. Pens, markers, crayons, pencils: the table is piled with all kinds of things. Maybe someone is doing a class project.

"Sit down," Skye says. She scoots along the bench, as if to make room. She tucks her scarf tail into her lap. The mittens and scarf are apparently an everyday thing.

"What are you doing?" I ask.

She motions at me. "Sit down."

This does not compute. "I eat over there," I remind her. My usual table is waiting. Empty, lonely. "See you later."

Skye sighs heavily as I walk away.

I slump into my usual seat. Skye clatters her tray down across from me.

"Chester Keene, you are not an easy person."

"I know." The sloppy joe sauce is soaking through the bun more and more by the second. Why won't she just let me enjoy my sandwich in peace? "What are you doing?"

Skye spreads the pile of clue cards out on the table. They look a bit the worse for wear, as if they've been jumbled in the bottom of her backpack since yesterday. "We have work to do. Hello?"

I reach for the #6 clue to refresh my mind. Smooth it out and dust the crumbs (crumbs?!) off it.

> Your next treasure waits in a honeyed box
> With a trio of bears and golden locks.
> Something borrowed, something blue,
> a lucky lane and the number two.

"We're still not sure what *the key to the hive* means, either."

"Wasn't it about the bee? We had to move it to get to the Flash."

"It might have another meaning," Skye says. "Clues often do double duty. Especially since the new clue mentions honey."

"We shouldn't backtrack," I say. The new clue is what matters most. I'm sure of it.

Skye recites the special words. *"Borrowed, blue.* Like from a wedding?"

"What would a wedding have to do with anything?" I ask.

"It's a bride thing," Skye explains. "You're supposed to carry something old, something new, something borrowed, and something blue down the aisle. For good luck."

"Oh. Well, I don't think either of us is getting married anytime soon, so . . ."

"Yeah, not us, but . . ." Skye looks thoughtful. "Dad might

be thinking about it. He's over the moon. They're all smoochy smoochy all the time." She rolls her eyes. "Even my mom says Dad's a goner. Totally in love."

"Yeah, I know what that's like," I admit, then push away the thoughts of Mom and Christopher. "Do your parents get along?" If Skye gets to see her dad, and even her mom gets to see him, his life as a spy must be a lot different from my dad's. He's safer. How?

Skye strips off her mittens and lays them on the table. "They've been divorced forever. They get along fine. They're just not a good couple. My mom works twenty-four seven and she's happier that way. My dad wants an actual life, whatever that means." She daintily picks up her sandwich.

"An actual life," I echo.

"Whatever that means. That's what they used to fight about. Not living together, they never fight. It's better." Skye slams her face into her sloppy joe. Forget dainty. She takes three giant bites, leaving a tomatoey trail all the way along her cheeks. What a mess.

Focus on the clues. Don't look. Don't look.

"Here's a napkin." Giving her one of mine is no problem. I always take six, even though it is always too many.

"Great." Skye takes the napkin and fluffs it open. She tucks it into her collar. No, no, no. She goes in for more bites.

Focus on the clues. Don't look. Don't look. But Skye has

inadvertently given me an idea. Speaking of things that gross me out . . .

"You don't think it means number two, like . . . you know."

"What?" Skye's huge red sloppy joe smile reminds me of the Joker from *Batman*.

I glance around furtively. "Like, in the bathroom. You know . . . number two?"

She shakes her head. "What are you talking about?"

"You know." I lower my voice. "People say number two so they don't have to say . . ." How does she not know this?

"Say what?"

I whisper. "Poop."

Skye cracks up. "I just wanted to hear you say it."

"Not funny." I cross my arms and glare at her. "It's really not mealtime conversation."

"I don't think the clue is about poop." Skye fairly shouts the word.

"Shhh."

"No one cares if I say *poop*. Poop!" She smacks my shoulder. "Except you."

"And anyone with a sense of decency," I mutter.

Skye cups her hand around her ear. "What's that?" I know she heard me. This is what she thinks is funny.

"We have to solve this."

"We will, Chester," Skye says. "Between the two of us, we know everything we need to know."

"How can you be so sure?"

"They wouldn't give us a problem we can't solve." Skye sounds so certain. Still, I'm worried. This task is stranger and more complicated than ever. Dad may be in worse trouble than we know. Every wasted minute is a new layer of danger.

18

THE KEY TO THE HIVE

Skye joins me on the bus again. It's weird, riding with someone sitting next to me. I have to put my backpack on my
lap and sit up straight. She chatters nonstop, too. She flails
her arms and the too-long sleeves of her blue jacket flop
over her arms. She keeps pushing them up, but they flop down
again right away.

The bus lumbers through the Alexander Street inter-
section along Dodge Avenue in front of the mall.

Observation: A giant clue, in the form of a giant sign, has
been hanging in my face the entire time. How could I have
missed it?

"I have an idea about the beehive thing," I tell Skye.

"Oh, yeah?"

"Come on, I'll show you."

The bus stop we use is on Dodge, right between the mall parking lot and the turnoff to my neighborhood. We get off and walk along the sidewalk heading away from the bowling alley, just far enough that we can see past the bulk of the mall.

"There's this place over there." I point across the parking lot. "Called Honeycomb Storage." The giant beehive sign above the warehouse winks in the afternoon light.

"Chester! That's genius!" Skye leaps with excitement. "Let's go!"

"We have to check in with Amanda first," I tell her. "Otherwise she'll worry."

We breeze through the bowling alley long enough to drop off our backpacks. "We're going for a walk," I tell Amanda. Her smile is much too satisfied.

I lead the way across the parking lot to Honeycomb Storage. We stand under the big beehive sign.

"Let's search it," Skye says. "Maybe there's a clue."

There isn't. We poke all over the pole, everywhere we can reach. Skye even climbs up on the base and feels around above our sight line.

"Well?" I say.

"Well," Skye says. "I guess we go inside?"

We walk toward the sliding glass doors. Skye slows to a stop on the sidewalk before we enter. She stares up at the sign over the door.

"I saw this logo somewhere yesterday. I guess it could have been here." She pauses. "But I think it was smaller."

"Were you over here yesterday?"

"No," Skye says. "I hung out with you and then I met my dad for dinner."

"Wait." My brain kicks into gear. "There's an extension of Honeycomb inside the mall. Maybe that's what you saw?" I'd forgotten about it until Skye said something.

"Yes! With smaller lockers!"

"That's more likely to be our target."

"Let's go!" We scurry back across the parking lot toward the mall. We skirt around the entrance to the big-box store. The main entrance around the corner offers a more direct route to the concourse.

The huge sliding glass doors separate as we approach and mall music comes pouring out. The interior hallway is two stories high and always decorated for the season. A retail cavern.

Immediately you have to make a choice: go up the double escalator, which leads to the main concourse on the second floor, or follow the flow of hungry shoppers toward the food court.

I never use this entrance. It's far from the bowling alley, for one thing. Also, the double escalator brings you face to face with the clock woman. There's no avoiding it.

We step on the escalator and I avert my eyes.

"Oooh," Skye says. "I love the view of her from this angle."

Even though I'm not looking I know what she sees. The massive wooden clock carved in the shape of a woman. She cradles the clock face in her arms like a baby, looking down at it with love. The sculpture itself is fine, if a little dramatic. But the clock itself has been stuck at 4:24 for as long as I can remember.

"It's been broken for years," I say. "I can barely stand to look at it." It's creepy, the way she's gazing at this damaged thing with such affection. They've balanced a seasonal crown of flowers on her head, which makes it even creepier.

"It's so beautiful," Skye counters. "I love her."

It isn't surprising that Skye likes something so weird. A thing that drives me nuts. I have a feeling that if we're going to be friends this kind of thing is going to keep happening . . . Are we going to be friends?

"There's something sad and timeless about her." Skye laughs. "Get it? Timeless?"

We're not done talking about the clock? "I like to know what time it is," I answer.

The treads of the escalator glide us up and up, until the moment the teeth at the top of the stairs ripple under the soles of my sneakers. Leap! Skye does the same. We bump into each other as we scurry past the broken clock woman.

"You won't even look at her?"

"It makes me sad," I tell her.

"Yes, she looks heartbroken." Skye's voice is appropriately reverent.

"I meant, it's sad that they don't bother to fix the clock," I said. "People need to know what time it is."

The second-floor concourse at the mall is lined with small shops on each side. The shops have weird and punny names: A perfume shop called Uncommon Scents is right next to an athletic shoe store called The Game's A Foot. The candy store is Nutcracker Sweets. A Rock for the Ages glitters with all kinds of jewels behind glass. Farther down the row is Remember the Mane, whose windows are an explosion of horse and unicorn paraphernalia: posters, stuffed dolls, enough glitter and rainbows to dazzle anyone into submission.

In the middle of the aisle, there are kiosks selling things like sunglasses, perfume, monogrammed snow globes, and sports team apparel. It's all one long runway leading to the department store at the end of the hall.

We stroll past the Roadhouse diner. The known spy hangout. I can't help but crane my neck. Maybe Dad is in there. Would I recognize him? Probably. Mom has a few pictures of him in an album. She doesn't like to look at them, but I do. He'd be older, that's all. Unless he's changed his appearance for a mission.

"There." Skye points at the hanging beehive symbol. It's two storefronts away.

"Hi," the clerk says. "Need a locker?"

"We have one already." Skye's voice carries so much confidence. We stroll right in, among the rows of yellow-painted lockers. *Honeyed box,* indeed.

Each locker has a colorful picture on it, a scene from a story. Some come from old fairy-tale classics: Cinderella, Snow White, Goldilocks and the Three Bears, Jack and the Beanstalk, alongside images from modern stories like *Frozen, Moana, The Incredibles.*

"It's a cartoon bonanza," Skye muses, studying the pictures.

The clerk says, "People would always forget their locker number. They remember the fairy tales. It's the darnedest thing."

Each locker has an electronic keypad, similar to the ones outside the laser tag arena. A four-digit code will unlock it.

"With a trio of bears and golden locks," Skye recites, positioning herself in front of the Goldilocks and the Three Bears image. It also happens to be locker number six.

"Six is my lucky number," I say.

"Is that why we bowl in Lane Six?" Skye says. "Is that your lucky lane?"

"Yes!" I see where she's going with this. The last two numbers must be six and two.

Something borrowed, something blue.

"Your jacket." I tug on her sleeve and she turns around. ALI 24-0. "Didn't you say this was your mom's?"

"That would be two-four-zero-six-two," Skye says. "But it's only a four-digit code."

"Let's try two-four-six-two," I suggest. "Zero doesn't count."

"Zero totally counts! It's a number just like everybody else."

I don't even know how to respond to that.

"But you're probably right," Skye continues. She punches in my combination guess.

The locker door pops open.

19

THE CLOCK WOMAN

"Chester wins his bets," Skye says.

I smile. "It was a team effort."

The locker is empty, except for the next folded card, marked with a 7. The Honeycomb clerk observes us with interest as we huddle together to read it.

> Slim is the chance of success in play
>
> when the lady won't give you the time of day.
>
> You will gaze upon her frozen face
>
> on the path to one sweet victory place.

"Sweet victory," Skye repeats. "Maybe this means we're close to the end."

Maybe. Meanwhile, my limbs tense up.

"We could go bowl while we think about it," Skye says.

"I have to do my homework," I say. The sudden strong desire to return to my routine hits me like a wave.

Time of day . . . frozen face . . . It's pretty clear to me what the clue must be about.

Maybe Dad doesn't know how much the clock woman scares me. I don't know if I ever told him. Why would it come up? It's something I avoid. Or maybe he wants me to face my fears.

Breathe. Be brave, for Dad.

"I think I know," I tell Skye. She follows my lead back onto the concourse.

The clue says specifically to gaze upon her face. Ugh. It's been forever since I looked at her face, and yet I can still see it in my mind.

Keeping my head lowered might be possible. We search around the clock's base. The carving is really quite intricate. The bottom half of the lady is carved like a tree trunk. She's not a grandfather clock, and not a grandmother clock either. She's something all her own.

"I see it," Skye announces. "Way up there."

She's pointing exactly at it, probably. I dare a peek. The corner of a card pokes out from behind the clock face, wedged between the metal rim and the woman's wooden bosom. It's all too weird. And way too high to reach.

Skye's outstretched arm falls about two feet short, and she's taller than me.

"Bump me up," she says. "So I can reach it."

"I don't know how to do that."

"Lock your hands like this." Skye interlocks her fingers so her palms form a cup.

"Pretend we're cheerleaders." She puts on a super-cheerful voice. "Ready? Okay!"

She sticks her DIRTY SHOE out at me. I jump back. I can't help it.

"Grab my foot and bump me up," she says.

"Yuck. Take off your shoe, at least."

Skye rolls her eyes. "Fine." She jams the toe of one shoe against the heel of the other and slips her shoe off. "It's no big deal."

Face my fears. Do it for Dad. No big deal. I lace my fingers, making the cup Skye showed me. I lock my elbows so my arms won't move.

Skye's stocking foot goes into my hands like a step. Her hands press my shoulders for balance and up she goes. She's not heavy. She's just . . . close. The front of her jeans ends up right in my face. Her shirt hem brushes my cheek as I tip my head away. Too close. Too close.

"Hold still. I almost . . ." Skye climbs up the side of the woman. "Got it!"

She drops down and steps away. I can breathe again.

Skye waves the clue card, victorious.

"Good job. What does it say?" I'm not about to touch the

card. There is still the residue of foot in my hands. My fingers splay out at my sides. They will stay like that until I can wash them.

Skye holds the card so we both can see it.

```
   Approaching now is an uncommon event
  Remember the names and follow the scent
 Toward troubling games, a treasure to loot
  Only teamwork can tackle the plan afoot
```

20

CARAMEL SURPRISE

We return to the bowling alley. First things first: I scrub my hands.

I'm fully lathered when the toilet flushes and a guy steps out of the stall. His movements in the mirror catch my eye. He's the skinny guy from the bowlers who were here yesterday, the one they call Ice.

He goes to the second sink. As he bends forward, his leather jacket rides up a little. Something glints under the fluorescent lights.

Double take. Did I just see what I think I did?

Blink. Focus on the soap bubbles carrying the germs away from my hands.

Can't help it. Out the corner of my eye, I peek again. Sure enough. Ice has a gun tucked at his lower back. Creepy!

"You keep scrubbing like that, you're gonna take off a layer of skin," he says.

"I had to touch something questionable," I answer. "Better safe than sorry."

Weird, that it's possible to have small talk with someone who's carrying a gun. I guess there are always people who have them, I just don't usually know about it. Which is maybe even weirder.

Ice shakes his hands and squeezes a paper towel between them. "Safety's overrated."

Not on a handgun. Luckily my head gets the better of my mouth and I keep that thought to myself. "Cleanliness is next to godliness," I answer instead.

Ice grins. "Stay clean, kid." He tosses his wad of paper towel into the bin and saunters out the door.

I know that Amanda prefers people not to bring guns into her place, but there's not a whole lot to be done about it. She's not going to get into it with the only paying customers on a slow day. So I keep this information to myself and rejoin Skye near the register.

"You need a snack?" Amanda asks us.

"We're open to snackage," Skye answers for both of us, even though it's getting close to dinnertime.

Amanda tips her head toward the office. "Butch brought cookies. They're decent."

"Yum, cookies!" Skye exclaims. "Homemade?"

"Uhhh," Amanda and I say in unison.

"Wait for it," I warn Skye as we go to investigate.

Butch is the lane wax guy. He secretly wants to be a baker. Or maybe it's not such a secret. Whenever he comes by, he brings a new thing he's made. It's never what you'd expect, like chocolate chip cookies or lemon bars. I wish it was. Butch long ago mastered the basics. He knows how to put a nice dough together. But he's convinced that the way to get ahead in the baking world is to be inventive.

Today's offering is labeled: *Macadamia Chunk Caramel Surprise.*

"They look great," Skye says. It's true. "Decent" is a pretty high Butch cookie rating from Amanda, too, so we dig in.

"The caramel's not really a surprise when you announce it in the name of the cookie," Skye says.

"The way it dissolves is surprising," I mumble. The flavor is good. The texture is not.

"Melt in your mouth," Skye chirps.

"And also in your hand . . ." After one bite, the entire cookie becomes a crumbly mash.

We fill out Butch's rating cards. He's left a couple beside the plate for us to make note of our opinions. Very scientific. Skye really gets into it. She hunches over the thing like she's taking an essay test.

We emerge from the office. Amanda has Lane 6 all lit up

and ready for us. Over in Lanes 1–2, Ice and his friends are mid-game.

"Why do you keep putting them all the way down at the end?" I ask while Amanda pulls out our bowling shoes.

"They asked for those lanes." Amanda shrugs. "They're a strange lot."

Today there's also a lone guy bowling in Lane 16. Probably one of the league bowlers, practicing in advance of the games tonight.

"Let's find Bubble Gum and Bluebell again," Skye says, reminding me that we named our bowling balls.

We scoot around the chairs toward the ball racks.

Thump-sliiiiiiiiide-crash! A whoop goes up from the grown-ups.

Skye turns to look. "Ice knocked down nine pins." The constant background noise of other people bowling is easy enough for me to ignore. Sometimes I forget what it's like to be new around here.

As we return with the balls, Skye announces, "Today I shall be Empress of the Lanes and Chief of the Royal Guard."

"You can't be both."

"Sure I can." She twists a couple of discarded straw wrappers into a crown and places it atop her head.

"The royal guard protects the princess," I explain.

"Empress," Skye corrects. "That's mostly so she doesn't

have to get her hands dirty. If they fail, she has to take care of business herself."

"I suppose." That made sense.

"I like being two things at once," Skye says. "Don't you?"

"I don't really know what that means."

"Warrior princesses are totally a thing. Let's be warrior princesses." She crosses her arms over her hips and draws two huge imaginary swords from imaginary scabbards. I lean backward as the blades whip out, so as not to be sliced in half.

"I'm a boy. I'd be a warrior prince." I rather like the sound of that, to be honest. My sword is held in a scabbard strapped to my back, like Link from *The Legend of Zelda*. I hold it aloft.

Skye assumes a fighting stance. "Or you could break free of traditional gender roles and become the princess you were always meant to be."

What? I lower my sword. "Ummm . . ."

Skye cracks up. "Your face! Your face." She doubles over. "It's okay. You can be a prince. Or the captain of my guard, if you want to."

My expression goes blank. I slide forward, until my face is close to Skye's face. "We are royal, and don't you forget it."

"We look innocent, but we're secretly tough." Skye holsters her swords, and so do I.

"Prince Chester of the . . ." She pauses, full of expectation.

"Neatly Folded?" I suggest.

Skye's expression lights up. "Prince Chester of the Neatly Folded and Princess Skye of the . . ."

"Sky?" It's the first thing that comes to mind. Ugh. Well, I'm one for two at least.

Skye sighs. "That's really too bad. You were on a roll."

There's a thrill in this spontaneity. "I can get it back," I say. "Princess Skye of the . . . Lightning Bearers."

She nods approval. "And those are our bodyguards." Skye thumbs toward the grown-ups a few lanes down.

A shiver courses over me. She's more accurate than she knows. "Yeah, they look tough," I say. Time to change the subject, otherwise I'll have to tell Skye the whole truth about Ice.

"That thing you said before about being two things?"

"Yeah?" Skye smooths her hands over Bluebell, ready to roll.

"I kinda get it," I admit. "My dad is black. My mom is white. I'm biracial."

"Me too," she says. "My mom is Japanese American. My dad is white."

"Is that why your hair is so perfectly straight?" I ask.

Skye laughs. "Um, I think that's a little bit racist."

"Really?" I say. "Sorry. I take it back, then."

"I mean, my hair is straight because of my mom, probably," she says. "You just shouldn't assume anything about a person based on their race."

"I don't think you should assume anything about anyone based on anything," I answer. "So that's fair."

Skye twists her feet against the floor like windshield wipers. "Yeah, baby. Bowling shoes are the best. Everyone should wear them all the time for dancing."

"It's kind of cool, though, right?" I ask. "That we're both biracial." There often isn't much I have in common with other people. Obviously I'm nothing like Skye in most respects, either.

Skye reaches for my hands. "Let's dance, then. A bowling shoes dance of biracial princesses." She winks at me. "And princes."

"Secret warrior princesses," I agree.

Skye smiles and twirls me like a contestant on *Dancing with the Stars*. Madonna's voice pumps through the speakers overhead and we bop to the rhythm, with the *thump-sliiiiiiiiide-crash!* of the grown-ups bowling adding a percussion effect to the music.

Skye sings along to the music. I don't know how she does it. There are still problems to solve, dads to save, homework to do, things to clean and things to worry about. And instead, somehow, we're living in the moment. For a few minutes, we are magic.

INBOX: ZERO

The magic ends at 5:04 p.m., when Skye leaves and I'm alone in Amanda's office waiting for Mom. There's nothing to do but worry and wait. The upbeat eighties music is still playing, one of many heavy things hanging overhead.

There's nothing in my email, still. Inbox: zero.

It's so confusing. Why would Dad come here, and be so close, but not just say what's going on? Is he unable to get to a computer? Is he being watched? Truly, the only way it makes sense is if he's in some kind of trouble. If these messages mean he's reaching out to us—to me—for help.

This time, Skye let me keep the clues. I collect them into a Ziploc sandwich bag so it's easier to keep them all together. As I read the latest clue over again, my stomach grows tight.

We never solved it. We barely tried. We got back to the bowling alley with the intent to work the clues, but instead all we did was dance and fancy bowl.

Troubling games . . . An uncommon event . . . The words turn over and over in my mind. My brain is set to Tumble Dry on High.

I'm not allowed to clean at the bowling alley. Amanda gets mad when I try. She always says they have staff they pay for that and then mumbles something about child labor laws.

Remember the names . . .

What names?

There's nothing I can do to help this stomach-knotty feeling except homework. At 5:09 p.m. I do my pre-algebra problem set, which is easy. At 5:28 p.m. it's my language arts essay, which is not. Mom will be here any minute. Gonna have to finish it at home.

"Chester, honey?" Mom's voice echoes from out there somewhere. She's probably catching up with Amanda. That's my cue to pack up my backpack.

My spy notebook is tucked in its usual spot. Yikes . . . I haven't written observations in it for two whole days. That has never happened. What is the matter with me? There could be all kinds of things going on right in front of me that I'm missing. This is why spies work alone—so they can focus.

Only teamwork can tackle the plan afoot . . .

What plan?

"Chester?" Mom calls, from nearer to the office now.

I jam the notebook away and shoulder my pack. Put on a good "everything's fine" smile.

Mom opens the door. "You ready, hon?"

"Yeah, sorry. Ready."

Mom smooths her hand over what's left of the bruise on my eye and cheek. It doesn't hurt anymore. In fact, at the moment it feels like the least of my problems. She kisses my forehead. "Let's blow this Popsicle stand."

"Roger that," I manage to say, even as my stomach tightens up like a fist.

This is really bad. We've taken two entire days just to get this far, and there's no telling how many more clues there might be. How long will it take to figure out our actual objective? In the first clue, Dad mentioned a prize at the end, but everything after that has started to sound more urgent. A plan afoot. Something we need to tackle. Does that mean something we need to do, or something we need to stop from happening?

One thing's for sure: this whole partnership idea is not working out.

Skye makes it too easy to get distracted. Every minute I'm not working the clues is a minute I'm letting Dad down.

FIGHT!

Two days' respite. That's all I get, and frankly, it's more than I could have hoped for. Maybe I jinxed myself by thinking that Marc Ruff-as-sandpaper had become the least of my problems, because on Wednesday before school, he's right there, waiting for me by my locker.

Oh, no. Oh, gosh.

Putting aside the ache of not knowing for sure, I try to imagine what Dad would do in this situation. Ignore, or engage? Ignore or engage? Probably I'm doomed either way.

"Hi, Marc," I say. Diplomacy is totally a thing in spycraft. "How is your week going?" The rest of my breath is frozen in my lungs.

His eyes narrow. Yup. Doomed either way.

"Loser!" he cries, throwing his arms up like he's thrilled

and surprised to see me. His voice is so loud and bursting that people around us turn to look. "What's good?"

He tosses a casual punch at my shoulder, like the cool guys sometimes do as a greeting. Only, his fist lands hard enough that it throws me off-balance, and my other shoulder collides with the bank of lockers.

My fingers tighten around my backpack straps. Ignoring doesn't work. Politeness doesn't work. New plan.

A dozen images flit through my mind in rapid sequence:

The sympathetic look from the whack-a-mole.

A Dad email: Bullies are secretly weak. Standing up to them is half the battle.

My hands on a laser tag gun.

Skye channeling Laila Ali.

"Fight!" A voice from somewhere beside me calls out. A rumble of cheers and interest rolls outward along the hallway.

Fight?

While my mind was going one way, my body went another. Right foot slid back at an angle. Left foot pointed forward. Bob and weave. Elbows bent, thumbs on knuckles.

"Whoa, whoa," Marc crows. "Look who's putting his dukes up." He laughs. Then his arm zips between my raised fists, quick, like a snake striking. No time to react. He grips some combination of my shirt, my armpit skin, and my back-pack strap, and with tremendous force, whips my entire body around him in a half circle, until my formerly-not-sore shoulder bangs up against the lockers that had been behind him a second ago. What the heck?

"Hey," yelps a girl, leaping back from her open locker. I smell raspberry lotion.

So much for my fighting stance. Where are my feet, even? Marc hauls me back the other way, jamming his fist into my armpit even harder. Dizzy, staggering, I end up turtled on my backpack, limbs sprawling, neck kinked.

Marc Ruff-cut stands over me for one terrifying second.

"Why me?" The words echo in my head, but apparently also slip out of my mouth.

"Why not?" he says. Then he's gone.

If a fight breaks out in the hallway, and no teachers are around to see it, did it really happen? All signs point to no.

It would be generous to call it a fight, of course. But that's the thing that's stuck in my mind, for some reason, the way someone shouted that out. As if I had made a good showing. As if I ever had a chance. The truth is, it only made matters worse.

Marc Ruff-patch will be gunning for me harder than ever. My neck aches. My shoulders feel all out of whack. There's a tiny rip in the seam of my polo shirt where the sleeve meets the body. The air smells rusty and my hands are cold.

"Are you okay?" someone says.

"Sure, yeah."

Brave face. No weakness. By the time the world comes back in focus, they're gone.

Other people rush around me; then the hallway falls suddenly and instantly near-silent. The homeroom bell rings, and for the first time ever, I'm not in my seat in class on time. I'm still walking, moving forward as if I know where I'm going. But I don't. My classroom is somewhere behind me. The classroom wings are arranged in loops, dipping out from the central foyer. From above, the school would look like a three-leaf clover, with the library at the heart. A fact that delights the librarian, Mr. Sands.

He's shelving at the way back when I walk in, but of course he hears the door open and the turnstile click. He pokes his head out. "Got a pass?"

"Yeah," I say. "I just need to look something up before first period."

"Right on." Mr. Sands disappears into the stacks without checking my nonexistent pass.

A thrill washes over me. Hiding in plain sight is definitely the peak of spycraft.

My reflection in the black glass of the computer screen surprises me. The rust smell? A slight nosebleed. Luckily I always have a few tissues in my pencil case. Doubly lucky that Mr. Sands was too far away to notice.

Inbox: zero.

Whatever. This is beyond an emergency. *New Message.*

> Dad? Please help me. I need you.

My throat tightens. I don't care if I sound pathetic or needy. This is what Dad and I do, right? We help each other. I'm doing my part, with the puzzles. Why isn't he?

> The guy at school I was telling you about? You
> remember. He's getting so much worse and I
> don't know how to stop him from attacking me.
> He's so much bigger than me. I got a black eye.
> And a nosebleed. And I don't know what next. I
> promise to try to learn boxing, so I can fight back,
> if that is what it takes, okay? But I need more
> advice. Please?
> > Love,
> > Chester

I pause. What I want to say next might be ill-advised, but I can't help myself.

> P.S. I'm worried about you. You never take so
> long to write me back. Are you in trouble? Is

there something more I can do to help? Don't worry—we're figuring out the clues as fast as we can. You can trust us. Just hold on, okay? Please stay safe. Please be okay. Please come see me as soon as you can.

Deep breath. No regrets. *Message Sent.*

"I had a brainstorm," Skye announces. She plops down at my lunch table, as if us eating together is an obvious thing now.

"Hi." Has she heard about the fight? Does she know? Even when things don't make it to the administration, sometimes word still gets around. Skye's face gives away nothing. Probably my suffering isn't worthy of the rumor mill.

"Hi," she adds, as an afterthought. "Let me see the clues again."

Lunch is pepperoni pizza. My hands are greasy and even though I took six napkins, like always, it's not time to deploy the second one yet.

Skye chows down on her own slice. "Well?" she mumbles. "Where are they?"

My sense of urgency wins over my sense of decency. I wipe my fingers on Napkin 2 and pass Napkin 3 to Skye.

"Don't get pizza on them."

"I don't have to touch it. I just have to see it," she says, jamming more pizza into her face.

The school napkins aren't exactly high-quality. Napkin 2 disintegrates beneath my hard scrubbing. It joins Napkin 1 in a pile of shreds beside my tray.

I pour the clues out of their plastic bag and spread them out on the table between us. The one we haven't solved looms largest in my mind.

```
Approaching now is an uncommon event
Remember the names and follow the scent
Toward troubling games, a treasure to loot
Only teamwork can stop the plan afoot
```

"There's some kind of plan," I said. "Something we have to solve and stop."

But Skye reaches for the previous clue.

```
Slim is the chance of success in play
when the lady won't give you the time of day.
You will gaze upon her frozen face
on the path to one sweet victory place.
```

"We already solved that one."

"But sometimes they come back," Skye reminds me. "Like how *key to the hive* had two meanings. We had to move the stuffed bee AND go to Honeycomb Storage Solutions."

"Okay. I'm listening."

"Slim, Lady," Skye says. "We know those names."

Right. The strange people who bowl in Lanes 1–2. I turn the card toward me. "What are all their names again?"

"Slim, Lady, Ice, and Sugar."

"Slim and Lady are part of the clue." It's right there in black and white. And there's more. "Look: *Frozen face. Sweet victory.*"

"Those could be hints that mean Ice and Sugar." The clue bears up Skye's theory.

"What do we do?"

"I don't know," Skye says. "For now, we eat." A knob of crust disappears into her mouth.

For a minute there, we were back on track. "We don't have any time to waste," I remind her.

Skye shrugs. "We'll figure it out. We always do."

"We should have been paying closer attention to them all along." The heels of my hands press my temples. My head aches, along with the rest of me. "What if we've missed important clues because we were too busy goofing around?"

"Chill out," Skye says. "We just got the clue. Now we'll pay closer attention."

"Ice carries a gun!" The words rush out. It didn't matter before. It matters now.

Skye's eyes light up. "Really? That's interesting. How do you know?"

"I saw it in the bathroom yesterday."

"And you didn't tell me?"

"Like you said, we had just gotten the clue. I thought they were random bowlers!"

"Random bowlers with GUNS? Please."

"One gun. That we know of," I correct. "I did think it was weird that they've been there two days in a row."

"Of COURSE they're part of the mission." Skye slaps her forehead as if to say *Duh*.

"They're planning something. We have to figure out what."

Skye shakes her head, amazed. "This is epic. He's really outdone himself this time." I'm not sure what that means, exactly. But there's no time to find out.

The warning bell dings overhead. Two minutes to the end of lunch. The thought of going back to class turns the pizza over in my stomach. Two hours and twenty-four minutes until the final bell.

And it's day three already. Whatever we have to solve, we have to solve it now.

EAVESDROP

After final bell, I race through the halls to my locker to grab my coat, and then beeline for the bus. Vigilance is the watchword. I'm taking no chances today.

Skye, on the other hand, is late. I'm still alone in my seat when the bus driver closes the door and starts to pull out of the space. My heart sinks. What am I going to do? But then he stops and levers open the door as Skye darts along the sidewalk toward us, waving and shouting.

"Thanks," she pants, tossing the driver a million-dollar smile. "You're a lifesaver."

Skye plops into the seat beside me. I'm very relieved to see her but when I open my mouth it comes out differently.

"You almost missed the bus," I snap.

Skye grins. "But I didn't."

"You have all the clues!" It's a struggle to keep my voice calm. "They give us ten minutes to get out of school before the buses leave. It shouldn't take more than five."

Skye shrugs. "I can do a lot with five spare minutes."

"You should always come straight to the bus!" My hands shake. Curling them into fists doesn't help. It's just a reminder of all the ways I've failed.

"That's no fun," Skye says. "I like to meet up with my friends at the end of the day."

"Who cares about fun?" The words burst out of me. "People are in danger."

"Don't be such a stick-in-the-mud," Skye says. "You take everything way too seriously."

"And you don't take things seriously enough!" It's hard to keep my voice down. Other kids on the bus are looking. Weird Chester being Weirder than usual. Whatever. My fingers trace the tiny metal lip along the base of the window.

Skye crosses her arms and looks out the windows on the other side of the bus. Probably just so she can turn her head away from me.

We take our time hunting for Bubble Gum and Bluebell. The balls get all mixed up after the leagues have been here in the evenings. It's a plausible excuse to poke around behind Lanes 1–2 for a while and listen to the grown-ups' conversation.

"Fido's still a problem," Slim is saying.

"He's no threat," Lady says. "I've checked him out. He acts tough because he's gotta, but he's soft. He'll roll over like he's supposed to."

"Fido's not the problem," Sugar barks. "Rover's the problem. It's all about the timing. Both doors gotta be open at the same time."

Slim sits easy. "The plan is solid. Quit yer yakking and get to the bowling."

"Oh my god," Lady gripes. She stares at her long manicure. "Couldn't we have picked a place next to a bar? Forty bucks I paid for these nails."

Slim chuckles. "Bar's right over there. Follow Sugar, she'll lead the way."

"Aww, screw you." Sugar sounds mad at first, but she laughs at the end of it. She looks toward the bar, all the way at the other end of the alley. "Don't mind if I do . . ."

Slim growls. "But first, flippin' BOWL."

"Forty bucks?" Ice tugs one of the belt loops on Lady's leather pants as she passes his chair, headed to pick up her ball. "Wah wah."

Lady grins. She wiggles her big round booty. Her voice goes high. Fake high. "Whatever are we going to do?"

Thump-sliiiiiiiiide-crash!

Skye nudges my shoulder, and I know what she means. It's suspicious if we hang around too close to them for too long. We move back toward Lane 6.

"They're going to steal something," I whisper.

"I think so too," she agrees. "Otherwise why would they be joking about money like that?"

"I don't think Fido's a dog, either," I say.

"It's whoever they're stealing from?" Skye suggests.

"Yeah." Now that we're on the case, I'm trying to breathe easier. Bubble Gum slides over my fingers like a familiar glove. I send it flying. One hard standard throw, nothing fancy. The force of my frustration behind it. Strike!

Skye cheers.

A few frames later, Lady and Sugar walk off toward the restroom. They slip past us without really noticing us.

"I'll be back," Skye says.

"Where are you going?"

She shoots me a withering look. "To the ladies' room," she reports. "A gentleman would know not to ask."

"I never claimed to be a gentleman," I mutter as she stalks away.

"Things to aspire to," Skye tosses over her shoulder.

For a while it is all guys on the lanes. Slim and Ice rock back in the seats, sipping water and beer. I run my hands over Bubble Gum's curves and think about my next style roll. Skye likes a mix of footwork, hip action, and upper-body moves. If I want to get out of the sixties in my fancy bowl score, I need to get more creative.

Skye comes back. The grown-ups resume their game too.

"Hope it all went okay in there." Clearly this is also something a gentleman would not say, but I do have a tough-guy image to cultivate.

Skye rolls her eyes. "I didn't really have to pee, dummy." She drops her voice to the barest whisper. "I went to *eavesdrop*."

"Eavesdrop?" I echo.

Skye clamps her hand over my mouth. I hope she washed her hands. "A little subtlety, please, Chester."

Her fingers smell like gardenia soap. Not fair. In the men's room, we have sandalwood. I'll have to talk to Amanda about changing it up.

"Sorry," I mumble through her fingers. They probably didn't hear me anyway.

"Don't you want to know what I learned?" Skye whispers. I nod. "You cn let go of mm fce."

"They're definitely up to something," Skye continues. "And whatever it is happens on Thursday."

24

SMOKE BREAK

"Tomorrow's Thursday," I whisper.

"Genius at work." Skye smiles to let me know she's teasing. We keep our heads close together to plan.

"What do you think they're up to?" I whisper. A mix of excitement and dread fills me. We've deciphered the clue, but the situation is growing more dire by the moment. Who are these people, really, and how does it relate to Dad? Could they be the ones watching or threatening him? Could they be the reason he can't contact me yet?

"Well, obviously . . ." Skye's voice rises to regular volume. I grab her arm. "Stealing something," she finishes on a whisper again.

"Yeah, but what?" I whisper.

Skye speaks loudly. "Do you still need help with your math homework?"

"Not math, language arts," I answer. I have a reputation to uphold.

"Right, the essay assignment," Skye says. She doesn't wink. She doesn't need to. It's like we're reading each other's minds.

It's too easy to let our voices rise. I pull a notebook from my backpack, and Skye and I sit side by side at the table, writing as if we're doing homework. We pool our knowledge.

Here's what we know so far. There are four thieves in the gang:

Ice. He's snakelike, wiry and tall. Very chill. Well named. He seems most likely to be the one in charge.

Slim. He's the poorly named, stocky one. Kind of a wisecracker.

Lady. Big hair. Big breasts. Long fancy fingernails. Whiny. (Skye says it's on purpose. She thinks the high voice is ultra-fake.)

Sugar. She's small, weathered, and coarse. She coughs like she smokes a lot. (Skye thinks her voice is real.)

The heist will take place on Thursday. Tomorrow.

"That's what we know," Skye says out loud. "It's not much, really."

"You're right. A good essay requires a lot more evidence than I've got."

"Ideas count," Skye muses. "But if you want an A, you need evidence."

The snippets of conversation we catch don't add up to much, except they must add up to something. We have one day to figure it out and intervene.

"Screw Fido," Slim bursts out at one point. "Why do we even care?"

Fido again, Skye writes. *I think they're talking about tying someone up.*

Who? I answer. Could Fido be . . . Dad? I gulp.

No idea.

"Why are they here?" Skye whispers. "Is the bowling alley a good place to rob?"

"Not really. We have a cash register, but look at this place. There's no one here." A guy tried to rob Amanda at knifepoint once. She hit him in the head with a bowling ball. He went to jail. That was a long time ago, before I can even remember. It's nothing but a story I heard her tell once. Maybe it's not even true. Knowing Amanda, it seems true.

"Is there a bank nearby?"

Hmmm . . . "Inside the mall. Two different branches."

"Isn't there a drive-through one in the parking lot?" Skye asks.

"It's way on the other side, though. It's tiny, like a kiosk."

"Just an ATM, maybe," Skye says.

"I don't know a lot about banks," I confess. "But that's what people rob usually, right?"

"Three fifty-five. Smoke break," Ice says.

"We should all go," Sugar answers.

"Affirm." Slim rolls himself out of the chair.

"Hang on," Skye whispers. "Didn't they go out for a smoke break yesterday at the exact same time?"

She's right. "Monday, too."

"Let's follow them!" Skye drums on my arm urgently.

"Wait, we can't just go out into the alley with them. Wouldn't that be suspicious?"

"Is it an alley out there?" Skye squints up her face like she's trying to picture the side of the bowling alley.

"Well, not exactly. It's the parking lot. And there's a row of stores over there. But it feels kind of like an alley because it's a dead end. The only place it leads is behind the bowling alley."

"We can go look. It's a free country, after all."

The image that pops into my mind is Ice, washing his hands and smiling, while the handgun peeked out of his belt. "It could be dangerous. We should be stealthy."

"Fair enough," Skye agrees. "We don't want them to know we're onto them."

"I have an idea. The dumpsters are out back." I point, behind the rows of pins. "We just need a cover story. Follow me."

RECONNAISSANCE

I lead the way over to Amanda. "Skye thinks I should be helping out more around here. I tried to explain that you have rules about things, but she doesn't believe me."

"I do have rules," Amanda answers. "Where are you going with this?"

"Can we at least take out the trash for you?" I suggest.

"Yeah," Skye chimes in. "This lump of a kid has clearly never done a hard day's work in his life."

That . . . might be laying it on a bit thick, if you ask me. But hey, we're improvising.

Amanda smiles. "Chester, don't think that just because you've got a cute girl on your arm you can trick me into letting you run the industrial vacuum."

My answering smile is genuine. That vacuum is the stuff of dreams. It sucks dirt out of the carpet, like, whoa. "We'll see," I tell her. "I'm not giving up."

"For now, just trash," Skye says. "We've got a bet going about it."

Amanda studies us. "Well, then." Pause. "Yes, on this special occasion you may take out the trash from under the counter here, and the one from the office." She reaches down and pulls the bag out of the basket. It's a small bag, but it works for our purposes right now.

"Just one is good for now," I declare. "Thanks!" We scurry away.

"Who wins the bet?" Amanda calls after us.

"Skye!"

"I do!" Skye shouts at the same time as we race toward Lane 1. Our improvisation skills are totally in sync. My body is buzzing, flying high on our success.

Skye makes for the not-really-alarmed emergency exit door that the grown-ups used.

"No, no. This way," I call. We scoot down along the very edge of Lane 1, toward the pins. We cross behind the threshold. Most people never see this part of the bowling alley, but it's actually pretty interesting. It's full of the machinery that makes bowling automatic. The pin setters, the elevators, the ball return wheel.

"Whoa." Skye is momentarily distracted by the sheer glory of it. No one's bowling, so not much is moving. It's still a lot to take in.

"Another time," I say. "We should get out there."

We burst out through the back door, into the actual alley that runs behind the bowling alley. It's pretty plain back here. Two dumpsters, a narrow expanse of pavement that's barely wider than a one-way street. A lot of miscellaneous gravel and other small misplaced rubble. There might as well be tumble-weeds rolling through.

Cautiously, we poke our heads around the corner. We have a full view of the three shops in the strip across the way. Discount Shoes is closest to us. The Haberdasher is in the middle. E-Z Check Cashing is down at the end, its big glass windows glowing brightly. Along the side of the bowling alley there is one row of parking spaces that no one ever uses. Ice, Slim, and Sugar stand in a cluster toward the front corner, puffing their cigarettes. Lady is nowhere to be seen.

"Three out of four," I say.

Skye opens her mouth like she's about to respond, but then several things happen all at once. Lady steps out the door of E-Z Check Cashing. Through the glass window behind her, Chet, in his cage, watches her go. An armored truck rumbles across the parking lot toward us.

"There she is," Skye says. "And—"

The armored truck stops in front of E-Z Check Cashing,

blocking our view of Chet. Lady waltzes along the sidewalk, coming toward the hood of the truck. The uniformed guard steps out from the passenger side.

"Well. Hi there, honey," Lady says, in her high drawl. "Aren't you looking dapper?"

The guard nods to her. "Good afternoon."

Lady totters off toward the front of the bowling alley. The other three thieves smoke and watch as the guard walks toward the back of the armored truck.

"The truck is blocking our view," Skye complains.

"Wait a second," I say.

The guard emerges with a wheeled, locked cart. He rolls it toward E-Z Check Cashing, disappearing out of our view.

"How much money do you think is in there?" Skye muses.

"I don't know," I say. "But there's bound to be much more tomorrow. People get paid on Fridays. Chet says it's his busiest day."

"Chet?"

"The guy in the cage."

Skye nods knowingly. "He's a friend of yours?"

"Kinda, I guess." Not sure if *friend* is the right word, but sure. "He's worked there as long as I can remember."

Skye nods again. "Hard to pull something like this off otherwise." She shakes her head in that way again, and whispers, "Epic."

"Something like what?" I ask.

Skye says, "So, Friday money is delivered on Thursday afternoon?"

"Why else would they plan the heist for a Thursday? They've been here all week."

Skye rubs her chin thoughtfully. "At least now we know their plan."

The armored truck rumbles toward us. The thieves turn to watch it go.

Skye and I scoot away from the corner, hoping not to be spotted. The truck curves past us, following its familiar path beyond the bowling alley and out of sight.

"Now we know their plan," I echo.

Skye claps, ultra-pumped. "Next we figure out how to stop them."

26

ANTICIPATION

Skye holds the dumpster lid open. I chuck the trash bag in there. Turns out we didn't really need the excuse. No one spotted us at all.

We stroll casually past E-Z Check Cashing. Chet is back in his cage, with the fresh cash no doubt secured in there with him. We wave. Chet waves back.

"We need a plan." I state the obvious, as we clump back inside through the front door.

"We can plan later," Skye says. "While they're here, we should observe them."

"We don't have a lot of 'later.'" Tomorrow's Thursday.

The grown-ups are pretty much done for the day anyway.

Thump-sliiiiiiiiide-crash! They finish their final frames with very little conversation.

"We don't even know how they plan to do it," I whisper.

"With guns, I guess," Skye speculates. "And tying the guard up?"

The grown-ups finish up and troop toward the exit.

"Didn't they stay longer yesterday?" Skye asks.

"Yeah," I answer. "They've been here after us both nights, I think."

Skye swings her fist down. "Dang. Why do they have to leave early now that we're onto them?"

"We know enough," I say, hoping it's true.

Skye looks determined. "It's up to us to stop them."

"We'll do it." We have to.

Somehow.

It's impossible to settle into my usual home routine, with thoughts of tomorrow looming. I pop a Tylenol and study the contours of my nose in the mirror. My face no longer hurts. My back, neck, and shoulders are still sore, but the ache is nothing compared to the anxious knot in my stomach.

While Mom is heating up the leftover meatloaf, there's a brief window for checking my email.

Inbox: zero.

A tiny flame of frustration surges in my chest. I wish Dad

would write back, so I could know for sure what all of this is about.

I roll my shoulders as the Tylenol starts to kick in, giving me a bit of relief.

This week has been so strange, but one thing is clear: with Dad around, it turns out I have the courage to stand up to bullies. Maybe that's what this mission is all about. He's showing me I'm tougher than I think. That I can handle more than I realize. That he trusts me to take care of a problem that is much bigger than Marc Ruff-neck.

I won't let him down.

If only he'd just told me that up front, maybe we'd have had more time to plan. Obviously the heist has been planned for ages, but we're only finding out about it now, and—

Wait . . . wait . . . my mind churns over a new thought. What if Dad is only finding out about it now, too?

At first, the clues seemed pointed. Like Dad knew exactly what was coming next and crafted the clues accordingly. But maybe he didn't. Maybe he had to buy himself time. Maybe that's why the clues build on each other. Dad needed to send us to places we could reach during the week. So he could keep sharing new information with us as he got it.

Maybe it isn't a wild-goose chase at all. Maybe all Dad had was rumors, hints, and clues himself. Maybe this is why he needed our help so badly, and why he couldn't trust that

I alone could break the code. It was all hands on deck. A crisis.

My brain clicks over the clues one by one. It all makes sense. The first clues pointed us to the storage locker, but it took us a whole day to get there. If the first clue had been "go to the storage locker," I'd have done it first thing after school on Monday. We might have gotten there too soon. The storage lockers get reset every twenty-four hours, according to the signs. Any abandoned items go to lost and found. Dad must have been at the mall on Tuesday to place the clue!

And he was clever. He managed to leave us a clue to the location of his next info drop, the clock, while also hinting at the identity of the thieves. The cryptic codes made sense, too, since the clues were hidden in public. They could have fallen into the wrong hands by accident. Dad would have no way of knowing if we would actually get to each one within the twenty-four hours.

But we did. We deciphered the code. *It's up to us,* Skye had said.

My heart thumps with this certainty. If Dad could simply call the police or stop them another way himself, he would. There must be more to this heist than meets the eye.

Whatever the gang of thieves is up to, we might be the only ones who can stop them.

THE PHONE CALL

"Chester," Mom calls. "Telephone!"

Her footsteps are already in the hallway. There's only time to flip up the end of my comforter to cover my spy notebook. I flop on top of it in a way that probably looks even less natural than it feels.

Telephone? For me? It rang a few moments ago, but it's not my habit to answer it. If Mom doesn't feel like picking up, we let it go to voice mail.

It's never for me.

Mom knocks on my door, then opens it. Privacy is a loose concept to Mom. "Telephone."

"For me?" It's all that's echoing in my brain. Could it be . . . ?

"Miracles do happen."

Hey. Is that a Mom dig?

She tosses the receiver at me. "It's Skye. Something about a project?"

"Oh, right. Thanks."

Mom backs out of the room with a smile. She closes the door again. I straighten out my comforter and smooth the elbow-shaped wrinkle out of my notebook pages.

Skye's already talking by the time the phone is at my ear. ". . . and then we jump out and stop them! What do you think?"

"Hi. What? You have to start over. I just got the phone."

"Oh, who have I been talking to all this time?"

"Yourself, I guess."

Skye laughs. "Yeah, that sounds like me. Anyway, I was saying I think I figured out how we can stop the robbery. We just have to interrupt them long enough for them to decide it's not worth it, and that they're more likely to get caught. They'll run away and we've saved the day!"

"Okay, yeah." I'm standing awkwardly in the middle of my room. Where do people sit when they talk on the phone? Desk? Bed? Floor? In the end I climb onto my bed and curl up against the wall with my back against my pillow. "So, we interrupt, we distract. They flee, we win."

"Yeah!" Skye cheers. "Unless what we're really supposed to do is catch them."

"Four grown-ups versus you and me? How is that possible?"

"I don't know, I'm just saying."

Whatever Dad needs, I want to get it right. "They'll have to somehow get all the money out of the armored truck and into their getaway car. Did we ever see what kind of car they drive?"

"No. But it must have a big trunk."

My stomach hurts. "They could've been planning this for months. We have less than one day."

"Yeah, but we're not trying to get away with millions of dollars or anything. We just have to stop them!"

Skye makes it all sound so easy.

"Listen to this," she continues. The phone erupts with the sound of sirens in the background, getting closer. "Sounds good, right?"

"What's that?"

"I found an audio clip online. We can use it to scare them off."

"Will that work?"

"I don't see why not."

There could be a hundred reasons why not. But Skye's confidence is infectious. "Okay," I say. "It's a plan."

"See you at lunch," she says, and hangs up.

THE HEIST

In the morning, when I rush out of the hallway toward the computer at 6:55, Mom's sitting at the kitchen table waiting for me. Huh.

"You're up early."

"Yeah." Mom strokes her Niagara Falls coffee mug.

So much for checking for a response from Dad. Guess I'll have to hit the library again.

Observation: When Mom sips from the mug, she tilts it up more than forty-five degrees. The cup is more than half empty. She's been up for a while.

Luckily, my bag is already packed and ready to go. It's stuffed to the gills: binoculars, utility belt, lockpick set, spy notebook—everything a person could possibly need to take down some armored car robbers. I hope.

"Honey, come sit with me a minute, please."

What part of *routine* does Mom not understand? Bowl, cereal, milk, spoon. A guy needs his strength on a day like this.

"Breakfast in a few minutes, okay?" Mom sounds serious. "We need to have a talk."

"I can't miss the bus." I'm already crunching a mouthful.

"I'll drive you to school today. This is important."

Whoa. "But you'll be late for work." Today is really not the day to disrupt my patterns. I have enough on my mind.

"I can be late for once," Mom says. "I'll just call in. I—I need to talk about what's really going on with you."

"What do you mean?" I keep on spooning the floating Os. Can't miss the bus, for real. Not today.

"I know you're not telling me the truth about what's going on at school," Mom says. "For instance, I got a call yesterday about you skipping a class? That doesn't sound like you."

Oh, that. "It's just a misunderstanding," I say. "I was in the library working on a project and ended up being late to homeroom. Someone called you?"

Mom shifts in her seat. "I shouldn't have led with that. I know you're a good student, Chester. But . . ." She breathes deep. "That's not all, honey."

Crunch. Crunch.

"I—I'm worried about what's going on for you socially. Is someone bothering you? Hurting you?"

My mouth is full, which gives me a moment to draw on my spycraft skills. Deception, deflection, de-escalation.

Swallow. "Mom, you don't need to worry."

"It's my job to worry. You came home with a black eye," she says. "And you know I value trust and honesty, but—" In the pause, she swallows hard. She rubs her forehead.

But you think I lied. My mind easily fills in the blanks. Mom knows, or thinks she knows. But what good would it do to confess? Mom can't teach me to fight. She can't protect me from Marc Ruff-day.

Observation: Her hands are trembling. Her eyes are red-rimmed. Just the thought that things might not be going well for me is stressing her out. The truth would knock her over.

"I value trust and honesty very much," Mom repeats, "but I know it's not always easy to live up to. I've done something—"

"So just trust me," I interrupt. "I have everything under control." Or I will, after today. With Dad in my corner, all things are possible. The thrill of what is ahead takes over. Mom's stuff can wait.

"Chester, I—"

My bowl slides into the dishwasher easy, just like how I slide toward the door.

"Chester, come sit," Mom says. "We really need to talk some things through, but I don't know where to begin. I need to explain—"

"Mom! Just stop!" Shoes, jacket, backpack on.

"Nope," Mom says, voice rising, body rising out of the chair. "You're not leaving until we talk about this."

"I can't miss the bus," I shout. "You won't understand my problems anyway! Just leave me alone!"

Mom stands in her bathrobe, fingertips pressing the rim of her coffee mug where it rests on the table, staring after me as I storm out.

Waiting through the school day is interminable. Also, it turns out that skipping homeroom not only gets noticed, it has consequences. My teacher says, "Chester, we missed you yesterday. But you weren't on the absent list. Is that a mistake?"

"Um. I was in the library finishing a project," I answer. "You can ask Mr. Sands."

My teacher shakes her head and hands me a hall pass. "You need to go to the office," she says.

Normally, it would horrify me to be called to the office. Skipping class is NOT how I usually roll. Please. I'm never even late.

Defying a teacher's directions isn't in my usual bag of tricks either. Today, though, I'm not the ordinary Chester Keene—I'm Chester Keene, the spy-in-training, and I've just been given a get-out-of-jail-free card. Instead of walking to the office, I click through the library turnstile. Mr. Sands is at the circulation desk. This time I have a real pass to hold up.

Deception, deflection, de-escalation. I'm on a roll.

Inbox: zero. Surprise!

Doesn't matter anymore. We're close now, close to solving this puzzle. Mom's big talk made me realize one thing, at least: it's stressful to have a lot of stuff you can't talk about, and even more stressful when people try to make you talk about them. People keep secrets for reasons. Maybe if I send Dad some reassurance that I get it, he'll feel better about reaching out in the ways that he can.

> Dad, I know there's something going on with
> you that you can't tell me. And that's probably
> why you haven't written me back. It's okay. I
> understand. I just want you to know that we are
> on the case. We have followed your clues, and we
> have figured out a plan. I won't say more, in case
> this message falls into the wrong hands. But we're
> ready. I'm not going to let you down. Somehow,
> everything will be okay, right? I love you. Chester

Thump-sliiiiiiiide-crash!

Everything looks like business as usual at the bowling

alley for a Thursday afternoon. Except it isn't, and we know it. Games are afoot. Thieving games.

Thump-sliiiiiiiiide-crash!

The wait is interminable.

We bowl in Lane 6. They bowl in Lane 1.

Thump-sliiiiiiiiide-crash!

We watch them. They ignore us.

Thump-sliiiiiiiiide-crash!

At 3:40, the grown-ups end their game. They all go into the bathrooms.

"Should we follow?" Skye's whole body is poised with the question.

"Too suspicious," I whisper.

"Do the bathroom doors lock?" Skye asks. "We could shut them in for the next half hour and we'd be, boom! Done."

"That would be brilliant," I agree. "Except the doors don't lock." You push to get in, too. The only handle is on the inside. We couldn't even stick a pole through the handle to block the door opening, like in a movie.

"Can we push something heavy in front of the door?"

"I like where your head's at," I tell her. "But anything we can move they can probably move easier." If we'd known yesterday that they'd all be in there at once, we could have brought tools.

Sugar emerges from the bathroom first. She's dressed all in black, carrying a slender black backpack. Behind her is another woman. Taller, slimmer, dark hair slicked back, clad head to toe in black leather. Sleek, like a whip. We double-take.

"That's not . . ."

Skye smacks my shoulder. "I told you her voice was fake. Everything was fake." The face belongs to Lady, but she's shed her long nails, her big boobs, her round butt, and the puffy blond crown. She's a different person entirely.

Slim and Ice emerge moments later, both dressed in the same type of uniform the armored car driver wears. They shake long jackets over their shoulders to conceal the outfits.

"Ninety-nine here we come," Slim says, cuffing Ice on the arm.

"It's on," Skye says.

We figure the robbery will be fast and efficient. Slim and Ice will overpower the driver while Lady and Sugar steal the money from the back. They'll have a car parked out front. One of them will run over and pull it around. They'll load up all the money and drive off with it.

Or at least, that's what would have happened, if not for us.

The plan is this: I will go out through the alley. Skye will go out the front door. When the robbery begins, I will distract the robbers in the alley. Skye will sneak up on them from behind. Skye will puncture the tires of their getaway car. Then she'll play the siren music. The robbers will be forced to run away on foot, leaving all the money behind.

"Let's go," Skye says. We slap hands and move into position.

SPYCRAFT, IN PRACTICE

Hiding in the alley feels better than anything has felt in a long time. Dad believes in me, is counting on me to be strong. This is my moment to shine. Plus, having Skye for backup makes it all the more exciting.

But it turns out there are a few flaws in our plan.

First, we forgot all about Chet. At 3:55, he walks to the door of E-Z Check Cashing. He pushes the glass door open, reaches up and adjusts the little tab on the spring to prop the door open. The robbers stand outside the bowling alley's back door, smoking. And watching. Just like they have every day this week. So clever.

Sugar stubs out her cigarette on the bowling alley bricks and crosses the street.

"Hey," she says to Chet.

"Hey," Chet says. "Come on in. It'll just be a minute." He strolls back toward his cage. He starts unlocking it with his ring of keys. Behind his back, Sugar pulls something out of her pocket. It's too small to see. But what happens next is big. And fast. Sugar lunges forward and suddenly Chet is on the ground. He holds his hands and feet together, struggling as if he's tied, even though I can't see any rope or anything.

Sugar must be very strong! She uses her backside to keep Chet's cage door open, and at the same time, she hauls his whole big self right into the cage. She closes the door behind them. Within moments, she's in Chet's usual seat, hands folded and smiling toward the windows. She raises her hand in a wave.

The armored truck rumbles up, two men in the front seat. It stops in the usual spot, blocking my view of Sugar. The driver has his hand up, as if waving back to her.

The driver stays in his seat with the engine running. The guard opens the passenger-side door and comes out.

Ice and Slim move faster than I expected. Guns raised, they charge on the truck. Boom. The guard flinches like he hit a wall. He grabs his neck, then slumps down.

Slim catches the open passenger door before it can swing shut. He fires through it. The driver face-plants into the steering wheel. Ice darts around the hood to the driver's side.

Slim hauls himself up into the cab. He reaches across the driver's limp body and opens the door. Ice is there and ready.

The door opens, Slim pushes the driver out, and Ice drags him in through the propped-open door of E-Z Check Cashing. It all happens in the space between the armored truck and the building. No one passing by would ever be the wiser.

I don't want to look, but I have to. On this side of the truck, the guard—is he dead? But there's no blood. No terrible explosion. A tiny arrow sticks out of his neck.

Lady ties him up with more invisible rope, right there by the side of the truck. It's clean and swift. She liberates his keys from his belt using some kind of tiny power tool. The soft whirring noise barely reaches me.

Any second now, it will be my moment. I wait. Ice's dart gun is so big, and the guard is so still.

Lady slides the guard's key ring over her arm like a bracelet. Slim comes down from the cab and grabs the guy under his arms. Lady picks up his legs and they hustle him into E-Z Check Cashing.

Deep breaths, I remind myself. *Any second now. Be brave. Be strong.* Dad's words, in my heart.

Except . . . the guard never made it to the back of the truck to open it. That was supposed to be our cue.

Any second now. Surely when they come back out, Lady will take the key to the back of the truck. They're all in the building together now.

My stance is set. Balance on my toes, ready to spring. My fingers grip the corner of the bricks. Watching. Waiting . . .

Slim and Sugar come out of the building carrying large pouches. They climb into the cab, with Slim in the driver's seat.

It doesn't go the way we thought. Not at all. No one approaches the back of the truck.

The cue is not going to happen now. Our attack will be out of sync.

It's hard to breathe. Ice and Lady come out of the building carrying more pouches. They toss them into the cab. Then they bound around the hood as if to climb in too.

They are going to get inside the cab. They're not stealing the money, they're stealing the whole truck!

My breath whooshes out in one big wave. No money transfer, no getaway car. We guessed their plot completely wrong.

Any second now, Skye will have to start the sirens on her own. If she figures it out in time.

Three of the four thieves are in the cab now. Only Ice is left to climb in. Once they're locked in their safe little box, there will be no stopping them.

It's now or never. For Dad.

I burst into the alley. "Hey," I shout. "Stop, thieves!"

It turns out that I am not a very big or scary distraction.

Ice has a gun and so does Lady. They are not afraid of pointing them at me. I succeed in distracting them from the robbery . . . but only for a moment. There are no sirens. No one runs away.

Ice's gun stares at me like a third eye, one that can see through to my soul and wants to take it. It's a blow-dart gun, I know now. But it doesn't matter. The sight of it freezes me. I can't move. Not to charge, like a hero. Not even to run away, like a coward.

Inside the cab, Sugar pecks at the screen of a small hand-held tablet. "We have five minutes," she calls. "Starting now."

"I don't have time for this, kid," Ice says. His voice is cold and gravelly. He's just a bigger bully. My feet slide into their fighting stance.

I summon all my courage and plant my feet wide on the pavement. My hands fold into fists. If they try to go, they'll have to go through me. "You won't get away with this." He moves while I'm saying it, I guess. Strong fingers grasp my wrist. My other hand grabs for the pepper spray on my utility belt, but Ice is too swift. He has both wrists now!

My shoulder pops as Ice binds my hands together behind my back. He uses something thin and smooth. It cuts into my skin. My wrists can feel each other's pulse.

The scream rips out of me of its own accord. Deep and strong and terrified.

Skye darts out from around the corner, as if to come to my aid. She's behind them. They haven't spotted her yet. She still has a chance. "Skye, run!" I shout.

"Let him go!" Skye races into the alley behind the thieves.

Lady scoops Skye into her arms. Like lightning. Skye goes

down. I scream again. Maybe Amanda will hear and call the police. But the bowling alley walls are thick brick, and she's probably singing along to the steady music. We're on our own.

"Four minutes," Sugar says. "Let's roll."

Ice wrestles me back toward the corner where I was hiding, as if he plans to return me from whence I came.

"My dad is going to catch you." The words pour out before I can stop them. It's a mistake, to refer to Dad. I can't blow his cover.

Ice's eyes narrow to slits. He studies me, snakelike. I expect his tongue to dart out over his chin at any moment.

Lady rushes up behind him, dragging a wriggling Skye. "What's the holdup? Pop 'em and let's get out of here."

Ice blinks. The snakelike wariness fades. "They're just kids," he says. "Get me the cuffs."

RECKONING

Humiliation is being zip-tied to a dumpster in an alley, after utterly failing to be heroic. Mortification is having to be cut loose by mall security and sitting in mall jail while they call your parents from the gray phone on the wall. This security guard must be new. He doesn't know Amanda, and so he didn't listen when we asked him to call her instead or let us go back in the bowling alley.

"My mom is going to kill me," I groan. How will I ever explain all this?

"I don't even know what my dad will say." Skye leans her head against the wall and sighs.

"Maybe they'll just be happy we're safe?" I suggested.

Skye gives me side-eye. "Right, they'll be thrilled about

the part where we went up against armed gunmen. Like, for real."

"Of course it was for real. What did you think?" We've let Dad down. Failed completely. My hands shake, and I grip the cool, grimy metal of the bench in our cell.

"I thought it was part of the game," she says.

"GAME? What part of stopping an armed robbery did you think was a game?"

"All of it." She shrugs. "I thought they'd have squirt guns, or whatever."

Dense. The girl is three feet thick in the head. Why does Dad have me working with her anyway? "Squirt guns? Spies don't use squirt guns."

She lifts her head off the cinder block wall. "I don't really feel like improv right now. I'm kinda still freaked out."

Improv? "Wait, what?"

We gaze at each other in confusion.

"What are you talking about?" she asks. "I'm talking about our scavenger hunt. I thought this was part of it. Obviously we took a big wrong turn."

"What scavenger hunt?" My pulse quickens and my skin starts to itch. I want out of this small room. I want to know what time it is. I want my mom to get here. I want my dad to be here too and safe—for us to be together, for him to know how hard we tried. And to explain what exactly he wants from us this time. In person.

Skye stares at me like I'm the thick one. "The scavenger hunt from Dad . . ."

"My dad is a government agent," I tell her, dropping my voice to a whisper. "A spy. His missions are top secret." I shouldn't even be saying this out loud, certainly not in a place where we might be under surveillance. But I'm confused. Skye and I are supposed to be on the same team. She should already know this. Why would Dad send me to her if she couldn't be trusted?

"Okay," she says. "So your dad does it like a spy game and my dad does it like a scavenger hunt, but whatever you call it, this time we're working together so they can give us tougher puzzles."

My skin crawls hard. I want to rub myself all over, but that would be weird. I cross my arms so I can at least rub my elbows.

A clattering ruckus sounds outside the door. "What do you mean, there's no footage?" The security guard's raised voice carries into our little room. "A whole armored truck doesn't just disappear. Which way did they go?"

The door opens. The security guard pokes his head in. "Did y'all see which way the truck went?"

"I don't know." We were tied up at the time.

Skye shrugs. He closes the door.

"How can there be no video?" she says. "There are cameras all over the mall, including the parking lot."

"E-Z Check Cashing has cameras too. But sometimes security cameras are fake. To trick people," I suggest. I saw that in a movie once. But we had walked past a whole bank of small monitors at the desk in the mall security office. Cameras were rolling somewhere.

The security guard opens the door again. Christopher bursts into the room behind him.

"My god," he blurts out. "Are you hurt?" Why would Mom send Christopher to get me instead of coming herself?

"Hi, Christopher," I say glumly.

At the exact same time, in the exact same tone, Skye says, "Hi, Daddy."

"Daddy?" I echo.

"Are you both okay?" Christopher loops his arms around Skye. She settles into the hug, leaving me outside their circle.

Daddy?

The room is practically spinning around me. "Christopher is your dad?"

"You didn't know?" Skye asks, her face nestled in the crook of his arm.

I don't have to answer. The answer is obvious. The gears of my mind churn, processing what has just happened.

"I—I thought your daughter was named . . ." He always calls her Ro-Ro. Which is short for, um . . . "Aurora?"

"Daddy!" Skye screeches, smacking him on the arm. "How many times do we have to go over this!" She turns to me, looking freaked out all over again. "All this time, you didn't know who I was? What did you think we were doing?"

Now the world is upside down. Backward. I have no words.

Mom rushes in. Sees Christopher, Skye. Sees the thunder on my face. She bursts into tears. "Oh, honey."

31

PUZZLE PIECES

I pride myself on my spycraft. I have practiced and practiced to become very good at what I do. To be good enough to some-day work with Dad, to help him. Given enough clues, I can figure out any puzzle.

Clue 1: Christopher is Skye's dad. That can't be a coinci-dence. But why? What would Dad want with Skye and Chris-topher? Did he send Christopher to keep an eye on Mom?

Clue 2: Skye mentioned Dad's clues in front of Mom and she didn't ask any questions. She wasn't even surprised. But how could she know? Has she been getting messages from Dad too, all along?

Clue 3: Mom won't stop crying. In the car, all the way home, over dinner. Her eyes are rimmed red and she keeps patting my hand and hugging me and gazing at me like I'm going to disappear in a puff of smoke, or explode or melt or something.

This isn't right.

Mom is sad. She's scared. Way too much to make sense, now that the danger is over.

Or is it? Maybe Mom fears the robbers will come back to eliminate us as witnesses. Maybe she knows more about Dad's situation than I do.

"Mom?"

"Yes, baby?" Her hands cover my hands across the table immediately. "What is it?"

I look her in the red-rimmed eyes. "How long have you been talking to Dad and not telling me?"

Her face folds and crumples, like a tissue. "Oh, Chester. I'm so sorry."

Clue 4: She won't answer my question.

It's hard to tug my hands away. She doesn't want to let go. She cries a little louder, and presses her fingers to her mouth. For one long moment, we stare at each other, and nothing in the whole room moves.

Then Mom uncovers her mouth, about to speak.

The phone rings.

We don't move at first. It rings again. There's always voice mail. Except . . . the most important person who could call tonight wouldn't leave a voice mail.

Clue 5: Mom lets me take the call.

Usually, when you do something so bad you end up arrested, your parents take away things like phone privileges. It's never happened to me, but I've heard other kids at school complaining. Maybe that form of punishment wouldn't occur to Mom.

"Hello?" Every fiber of my being hopes it will be Dad, with an explanation for everything.

"Chester. Oh, my goodness," Skye gushes. "Can you believe this?"

Of course, it isn't really a question. It's part of a monologue in which Skye performs and I play the part of her unwilling audience.

"This is so immense. Dad said not to call you, but I just had to. I had to! Are you okay?"

When I don't answer, Skye keeps pouring out words. "Are you upset? You seemed really upset. I hate that you're upset. I didn't know you didn't know. I mean, I figured it out right away—how many Chesters can there be in the world, right? Geez, Dad can be so dense. He refuses to call me Skye even though everyone else in the world totally gets it. So, like, of course you didn't know. And it was super unfair of him to set us up like that without being sure you would get it. I'm really sorry." She pauses long enough to take a big breath. "But now that you know, it's so cool, right? The best game ever. We have so much to discuss, don't you think?"

My mind spins and spins.

Unfair of him.

Set us up.

Game.

"And the best part—did you realize it yet? The best part is, we were wrong about the robbers. I mean, the robbers were real, but that wasn't our clue. So we get to keep playing! We still have to solve the actual puzzle. See you at lunch?"

Suddenly there's silence. It's my turn to speak but I have no words.

"Chester?" Skye is waiting.

"What do you mean, that wasn't our clue?" My heartbeat speeds up, just when I thought my whole heart was about to fade to nothing.

"The scavenger hunt is still active. There's more to our quest!"

Then . . . Dad is still in danger. The weight on my shoulders is crushing. "But . . . what if we're out of time?"

"No, Dad says there's plenty of time. We can work on it again tomorrow! At school." Her voice is suspiciously upbeat.

Dad says. She means Christopher. And he knows what the clues point to? So it's been Christopher and Dad, working together to bring Skye and me into their spy mission? Why, if there is nothing urgent? If Dad's not in peril, why can't he just come talk to me?

The knot in my stomach says something isn't right. Skye and Christopher both sound super calm and not stressed at all. It's only Mom, like me, who seems worried sick.

"I have to go." I hang up the phone and turn slowly to face my mother. She sits perfectly still, except for the tears rolling down her cheeks.

"Mom. How long have you known?"

THE TRUTH

Mom's all choked up. I know she can't help it, but it's kind of annoying when I just want her to answer my questions. "What do you mean, sweetie?"

She's deploying an unusual amount of *honey*s and *sweetie*s, too. This can't be good.

"How long have you known that Dad is back?"

"Oh. Um." Tears. All the tears.

"Mom!"

"Sweetie—" Mom fumbles with her little mound of used tissues. She finds one that's not entirely balled up . . . and she reuses it.

"Mom, gross." I bring her a plastic grocery bag from under the sink.

She sweeps the pile of tissues into the bag and hangs it

from the knob of the chair. "Chester, go on and get ready for bed, okay? Then we can talk. I need a minute to think."

How is it bedtime already? A second is always the same length as the second before, and yet it feels like the world is spinning faster and faster. I'm losing time. Dad, too.

We failed and Dad is still in danger.

In the doorway, I pause. "You wouldn't need time to think if you were going to tell me the truth."

Floodgates. I leave Mom sobbing at the kitchen table, which feels kind of bad. I don't like it when she cries, which isn't very often unless we're watching TV. She loves to cry at TV, but that's different. It's not real. I mean, the tears are real, but there is a boundary around them. It's clear why they've come and it's clear that they'll be gone again, as soon as the credits roll or a funny commercial comes on. This is different. It's like a faucet opened somewhere, and I don't know where, and I don't know how much is left in the pipe or how to turn it off.

Clue 6: Mom did not deny knowing about Dad.

My backpack is still loaded down with all my spy equipment. Once everything is spread out on the bed, it's easier to think about what I'll need tomorrow. I pull the bin of Dad gifts out from under my bed, too, so everything is visible. We'll be working the clues again, so maybe my book about code breaking? Maybe *not* the binoculars—they're heavy and they haven't come in handy much lately.

Mom knocks on the door, then opens it. Her eyes are dry, but still red. She folds her hands over her stomach and moves toward me. But she draws up short in the middle of my rug. "What's all this?"

"I'm just getting my stuff ready for tomorrow," I say. There's no need to hide it from Mom now, since she clearly knows more than she has ever let on.

"That's not school stuff." Mom frowns.

"We still have to solve Dad's clues," I explain. "So I'm gonna need my tools."

Mom's brow wrinkles further. She holds her arms tighter to her stomach. Then her face opens up—like, aha!—and she presses trembling fingers to her mouth. "Oh my god."

She reaches behind her and closes my bedroom door. Which is weird, because there's no one else here. Then she's pushing aside my spy stuff to make space to sit on the bed across from me. "Chester, I—"

Her weight on the edge of the mattress causes my binoculars to slide into her hip, lenses first. Scratch risk! I rapidly adjust the things she's moved, so nothing gets messed up. Mom waits to keep talking until I'm done.

"I think there's been a terrible misunderstanding," she continues. "I've made a big mistake and I'm so, so sorry. I can explain." Mom takes a deep breath. "The notes and clues you've been getting this week are not from your father, they're from Christopher."

"Okay," I say. "But how does he know about Dad?"

"Christopher doesn't know anything about your father."

"But—" My brain struggles to rewind. Back, back, back to the point where I made a wrong conclusion. A faulty observation.

"He was nervous about introducing you to Skye," Mom says. "You're very different people and he knows that you can be shy about making new friends, but solving puzzles is one thing you and Skye both have in common. He thought it would be fun for you to be able to meet each other without the awkwardness of parents looking over your shoulder."

The truth settles over me. "Christopher made up all those clues? Just for fun?"

"Yes, honey."

"They're so clever," I said. "I really thought it had to be Dad."

"Christopher makes a scavenger hunt for Skye every year around her birthday. He's been working on it for weeks. It's their special thing, and he was really excited to include you in it."

All I can do is nod. There's a feeling in my stomach that

I don't know how to name. A softness, a sinking. Like a knot being untied, or a breath being let out. *Say it out loud, to make it real:* "The clues never had anything to do with Dad."

"No, sweetie. I'm so sorry."

Dad's okay. A smile bursts out of me. The feeling in my stomach? It's relief. Dad's okay! He's not in danger. He never was. He doesn't need my help. He's not even here!

He's not here. The sinking relief becomes a cavern inside me. I'm becoming so empty, it's almost painful.

"I've been waiting to hear from Dad," I blurt out. "So the timing, I just thought, I hoped . . ." I *wanted* the notes to be from him. But they weren't. He's probably off on a mission somewhere, and he hasn't even seen my emails. I've been so foolish to think that he would come for me, after all this time. That he could really be here.

My gaze drifts to the closed bedroom door. *There's no one else here.* Is there?

I leap up and race to fling the door open. "Dad?" I shout. The hallway is not that long.

My eye goes to the front door lock, standing at a vertical angle. Unlocked! It's never unlocked. A tiny flutter of the window curtain draws me toward it. Sure enough, there's a shadowy figure walking rapidly across the driveway, away.

"Dad!" I shout again. But now Mom's in the room with me. "Is that him?" I spin toward her. "Was he here?"

My feet slide into my shoes, but my fingers fumble the laces.

Mom blocks the door with her body. "Chester! Your father is not here," she says. I grab at her, desperate to move her aside. Maybe I can still catch up to him!

"Then why is the door unlocked?" She's still in my way, holding me back.

"I—I don't know," she stammers. "We were both upset when we got home. We must have forgotten."

"We never forget!" I insist. It's part of the routine.

"Chester, please." Mom's voice catches. "Your father's not here, and he's not coming."

"You can't know that for sure."

"Yes, I can," Mom says firmly, her fingers fumbling for the door bolt. It locks with a metallic clunk. "It's not Dad who's been sending you those emails. It's me."

CONFESSION

For a moment, it's quiet. Then the laughter bubbles up from inside me. It echoes off the walls of the canyon inside me, making it sound like a hundred Chesters laughing. It rumbles my chest.

When I can breathe again, I say, "You had five minutes to think, and that's the best you could come up with?"

"I'm sorry, sweetie," Mom says. "I never meant for it to go this far."

"You're covering for him," I say. "What's really going on? Where is he?"

"I have no idea," Mom says, her hands on my shoulders. "As painful as it is, he left us."

"People don't just disappear," I argue. "Lots of kids have separated parents, but they know where they are."

Mom takes me by the hand and pulls me away from the door, toward the couch. She perches on the edge and pats the cushion beside her.

No way am I sitting. "Tell me where he is. Tell me what you know. Is it his work that keeps him away? It is, right?"

Mom shakes her head. "I really don't know."

His work for the government took him away from us. It's the only explanation that makes sense. For why he wouldn't be able to stay in touch, but still care enough to send presents.

"There has to be a reason. He loves me! He's told me. And he never forgets my birthday."

Mom swallows hard. "There's no doubt in my mind that wherever he is, he loves you. In his way." She shakes her head. "He's just . . . he's not someone we can count on. And I'm so sorry about making you think otherwise."

My head is spinning, my stomach churning. "What are you talking about?"

"You've been having trouble with a boy at school," Mom says. "You've been really upset, sometimes even scared, but you won't talk to me about it."

My heart beats fast, like I've been running and now I'm caught. "How do you know that?"

"The email address you found after your birthday is an old one of your father's. When we were together, we used it as the login account for a variety of things online. Streaming, shopping."

"Like how he uses it to send my gifts," I say. "That's how I found it."

Mom nods, twisting her hands together in her lap. "Yes. But your father doesn't check that email anymore. It was just a fluke that I managed to see your first message."

"So, you've been reading our emails?" Mom's own form of spycraft. Guess it runs in the family. The heat of embarrassment fills me. Those messages were private. I would never tell Mom those things. That was the whole point.

"Not just reading, sweetie, I—"

"You're lying!" I shout. She said it once, and I'm not going to let her say it again. I refuse to hear those words a second time. Mom knows things she shouldn't know, but that doesn't prove anything, except that she's a liar. "You just don't want me to see him or talk to him. You just want to ruin this for me!"

The computer is right there. Forget Mom's lies. I will send another message to Dad. One that demands a response. One that he can't ignore. And when he responds—which I know he will when he's able—when he responds, it will prove once and for all that he's out there. My fingers shake as they tap out the password.

Inbox: 1.

34

INBOX: 1

"Ha!" I shout to Mom. "See? He wrote me."

"That was earlier," Mom says. "Before the robbery. Your last note sounded so—"

"Just stop." I turn my back on Mom to focus on the message. "It's not going to work. You might not like Dad anymore, and he might have left YOU, but I still need him. You have no right to mess that up for me. There's probably a law about it or something," I declare.

> Dear Chester,
>
> It sounds like you're having a really hard time. That stinks. I did survive middle school, but painful things happened to me, too. You are so strong. You will get through it, just like I did.

Learning some self-defense is a good choice, but the first thing you'll learn there is that fighting should always be the very last resort. You don't need your fists to beat this guy.

Bullies are weak people who need to pretend they have power to feel okay in the world. He probably wants attention more than anything. Keep trying to ignore him.

Be a brick wall. He can't knock you down. Nothing he throws at you even makes a dent.

Be a mirror. Whatever he says to you or does to you reflects back and hurts him instead.

Be brave enough to ask for help. What is the name of the boy who is bullying you? If you tell Mom or one of your teachers what is going on, I am sure they can help.

The living room is quiet as I read. Mom's all the way over on the couch, sniffing into her thousandth tissue, and her presence looms large. It doesn't stop me from hitting Reply.

Dear Dad,
I'm glad you're safe. No, I can't tell anyone else. I can't even type his name here, because I don't want it to be seen. You are the only person I can trust.

Does he know Mom can see our emails? I don't want to tell him, in case it might scare him away.

> I tried ignoring him. I tried standing up to him. He just keeps coming. I don't know what I ever did to him.

Be a wall. More like, get thrown up against one. *Be a mirror.* More like, see my bruised face staring back at me. Dad's advice usually fills me with strength, but right now, it doesn't feel like enough. I need more. I need . . . proof.

> Dad, I really need to see you. When can you come? I know you're busy, but please. Please. Please. I really need you. Here. Thanks for listening.
> > Love,
> > Chester

It's possible to push back from the desk without turning around. "Don't read it," I say to Mom.

"Chester."

"DON'T read it." It's on the tip of my tongue to make her promise. But who can trust the promise of a liar anyway?

Mom says nothing as I disappear down the hall and into my room.

SALISBURY FACE

Now I know what it means to toss and turn all night. I'm usually a very good sleeper. There's a cloud over my Friday morning routine. The shower leaves me feeling less than clean. I brush my teeth in a funk, scarf my cereal in a daze, ignore Mom's presence in the kitchen with the focus of a tightrope walker.

To make matters worse? Inbox: zero.

In the library before school, still nothing. I take slow deep breaths and try to brace myself for another weeks-long wait.

"Booga wooga!" Skye dances toward me along the lunch line, cutting in front of a bunch of people. "Ready, Freddie?" She waves the bag of clues at me.

"No cutting," I say.

"Ooh," Skye says. "Someone's in a mood."

Wouldn't you be, after everything that just happened? Some things can't be said out loud. Many things. Can't forget that.

"I'm fine," I say. "There's still no cutting."

Skye turns to the people behind us. "I need to talk to Chester. Y'all cool?"

Noncommittal shrugs, a couple of grunts is all she gets in return.

"See?" Skye says. "It's cool. You worry too much. There'll be plenty of, um"—she consults the chalk-written menu as we round the curve into the serving area—"Salisbury steak and mashed potatoes to go around."

Ew. My second-least-favorite lunch.

Skye chatters away about the clues as we go through the line. Scavenger hunt clues. Meaningless clues. A game that won't get me any closer to anything. It's hard to tune her out, but I do my best.

We swipe our cards and step out into the main cafeteria. Skye walks ahead of me toward my table. Resigned to this fate, I fix my gaze on her two scraggly hair buns and follow. Too late, it occurs to me that Skye isn't taking the circuitous path. She leads me straight past Marc Ruff-side's table.

Oh, no. Oh, great.

Be a wall. Be a mirror.

Marc bellows, "Keene, this Salisbury steak looks like your face."

Ignore.

"Hey." Skye pivots, a fierce expression on her face. "Don't talk to him like that!"

Marc just laughs. "Wowee, look who's got a little girlfriend. What's she see in you, Keene? Or should I say Salisbury-face?"

It's like I'm outside my body. My fingers squeeze tight around the edges of my tray. The momentum comes from somewhere beneath or behind me, launching me forward.

Firm like a wall. Shiny like a mirror. My lunch tray goes vertical, smashes straight into Marc's face. Peas go rolling over his shoulders, down his arms, and onto the floor. Mashed potatoes smear in his hair and eyelashes and nostrils. Gravy drips down his cheek onto his shirt and the objectionable chunk of ground beef leaves residue on his stubble before it plops into his lap.

"Your face *is* the Salisbury steak," I declare.

Oh, no. Oh, crud. Oh, no. Oh, man. What did I do? My feet fly over the tile. All eyes are on me, fleeing the cafeteria. One goal: put space between me and Marc Ruff-start. There is not enough space in the world.

I'm dead.

He's going to actually kill me. So much for surviving middle school.

I've never moved so fast in my life. Out of the cafeteria, across the atrium, through the door, along the wide front sidewalk leading away from the building.

Oh, no. Oh, crud. Oh, no. Oh, man. What did I do?

The parking lot is full of teachers' cars except for an empty patch of long, angled lines where the buses pull in at the end of the day to wait for us. There's nowhere to go. A real spy would know how to hot-wire a car and drive it away, or be able to send a signal for a colleague to come pick them up. Or, they'd already have a getaway plan—a motorcycle out back, or . . . I don't know . . . a jet pack?

My only option is the city bus stop across the main road. The map on the wall of the bus hut says the 66 bus will take me from here to the bowling alley. The auspicious route number gives me a fleeting glimmer of hope, but it dissolves.

The cold of the metal bus bench hits the back of my legs, even through my jeans. My hands cover my face and my elbows rest on my knees.

Oh, no. Oh, crud. Oh, no. Oh, man. What have I done?

"You wanna talk about it?" says a now-familiar voice. Skye.

"Not really," I mumble into my hands. What is there to say?

"I mean, if you say we gotta throw down I'm gonna throw

down," she says. "No questions asked. But knowing why doesn't hurt."

Something light drapes around my shoulders, warding off the chill. The sudden slight warmth causes me to sit up and slide my arms into the sleeves of the . . . well, it's some kind of sweater. Very fluffy, very bright pink. Definitely an extreme statement piece within the landscape of my fashion sense. But very warm.

"Thanks," I say. The cold hadn't really hit my brain yet, but my body had definitely been feeling it.

"I'd hate for you to freeze to death before we solve our mystery," Skye says. "That would take some of the glow off the victory."

"Some?" My forehead wrinkles.

Skye says gravely, "Never underestimate the joy of solving a good puzzle."

It's weird that she's followed me. Weird, and nice. "What are you even doing here? You're going to get in trouble."

"I'm impervious to trouble." Skye waves a mittened hand. "It's a gift."

"Yesterday notwithstanding."

"Eh," Skye says. "Would we call that trouble?"

I don't even know what to say to that.

Skye grins and whips her scarf tail over her shoulder. "I guess now that I'm hanging around with you, I have to recalibrate."

"Sorry." I tug the sweater tighter. "I didn't mean to drag you into anything."

"It's no big," Skye says. "Come on. Let's get outta here before someone sees us."

It's a bus stop. What does she think I'm trying to do? Of course, I don't have any money or a bus card. All my stuff is in my locker. Mentally, I kick myself. A good spy would be ready for such spontaneity.

"I'm just gonna sit here and wait for my mom," I say. "But thanks for the sweater. Really."

"You called her?" Skye asks.

"Don't you think the school will call her when they find out what I did? And when they realize I'm skipping class?" There's no way I'm going back in there. Not now.

"Oh, you sweet summer child," Skye says.

I don't know what that means.

She thumps the top of my backpack. "Come on. We only have twenty minutes before the end of lunch."

Sigh. Well, it beats trying to figure out the bus routes to get to the bowling alley. And it definitely beats going back to school.

Skye's house is extremely close. It's in the nice neighborhood with the big brick houses that's practically right across the street from the school. She leads the way up the walk of a massive house with a glittering glass-and-brick front. It has two chimneys and a three-car garage. The driveway alone is longer than our entire apartment.

"This is where you live?"

"Yup," Skye says. "Home sweet home."

She dials a code on a keypad that opens one of the garage doors. Two-thirds of the garage is empty, and the other third looks like some kind of outdoor junk room. Skye swipes her feet on the mat and slips her shoes off as we enter the house into a sort of hallway that opens to the kitchen. With the punch of a button, the garage closes behind us.

We troop into the kitchen. Skye's first stop is the house phone hanging on the wall above a small desk at the edge of the counter. She dials.

"Hi, Evelyn, this is Mai Donaldson calling." Skye affects a slightly deepened, slightly annoyed-sounding tone. "I'm picking up my daughter, Skye Donaldson, and her cousin Chester Keene for dental appointments after their lunch period." Skye winks at me. "I just wanted to confirm that Skye delivered the note I sent to the office this morning. Last time, she forgot, and I got four separate calls about her skipping classes."

Pause.

"No record? I swear, that child would forget her feet if they weren't attached to her body. Will you add her to the list, please? I'm in court tomorrow, and I won't be free to respond to a bunch of unnecessary calls about skipped classes. Though I do appreciate your diligence."

Pause. I'm starting to get the feeling Skye may have done this before.

"Yes, Evelyn, one-fifteen," Skye says. "Yes, they know to come to the office and sign out. Let's hope they remember." Skye's fake tinkling laugh makes me smile in spite of myself.

"Evelyn, you're a dear. Buh-bye now."

Skye hangs up. I offer a small round of applause. She curtsies. "How's that for improv?"

"I didn't know people actually did that," I confess. "I figured it only works on TV."

"Now . . ." Skye stands in the center of the kitchen, hands on her hips, eyeballing me. "Chester Keene, you and I have problems to solve."

VOICE MAIL

"First things first." Skye swiftly makes two peanut butter and jelly sandwiches and pours out carrot sticks and SunChips for us to share. This is way better than Salisbury steak, in my opinion.

Skye perches on one of the counter stools and motions me to the other. "Hey, Babycakes?" She speaks to the small round digital assistant on the countertop. "Play us some nice sultry blues."

"As you wish, Glitter Girl," responds an electronic woman's voice. Slow swelling music begins to pump from hidden speakers.

"Arigato," Skye says.

"Anything for you, love," the machine says.

We eat in silence in a matter of minutes. I've never known

Skye to go this long without talking, even when her mouth is full. The respite from human interaction is nice.

When we're done, she leads me upstairs, over a landing, and down a hallway into her bedroom. The room is an explosion of color. Pale-purple walls, a textured white ceiling, two huge windows with bright purple-and-teal polka-dotted curtains. The walls are smattered with posters and drawings and photos and what appears to be a Hello Kitty dartboard. The bedspread is a cool blue fluffy-looking thing, scattered with shaggy pillows of all shapes and colors. A menagerie of stuffed animals tops the bookcase, which is overflowing with books and papers.

There's a massive purple beanbag, a rug that's a map of the world, and a desk with a laptop, a lamp, and even more stuffed animals on it.

"Have a seat," Skye says.

There's the bed. There's the desk chair. The beanbag. One of the windows is pushed out from the room, creating a deep window seat with a gray cushion, which is already occupied. A black-and-white cat snoozes in a ball of fur.

"This is Bartholomew." Skye scratches him under the chin. He lifts up his head to give her better access. "He's super old. We let him mind his own business."

I choose the edge of the bed.

Skye sits on her desk chair and swivels to face me. "So,

what's the deal with that guy? The C.K. I know doesn't go around smashing food into people's faces for no reason."

"C.K.?"

Skye rolls her eyes. "I really feel like you can crack that code, C.K."

"I don't really do nicknames."

"It's affectionate, you goof," Skye says. "Just deal."

"Okay . . . Aurora."

Skye shrieks. She grabs a mini stuffed animal off the pile on her desk and throws it at me. "You are forbidden to call me that. Only Dad is allowed, and only because I can't stop him."

"It's a pretty name," I offer. "Aurora Skye Donaldson."

"Look at this face." Skye frames her cheeks with her hands. "Do I deserve to be named after some insipid Disney princess, who spends half her own story passed out in a tower? Puh-lease."

"Also aurora borealis, the northern lights. They're pretty cool."

"Oh my god," Skye groans. "You've clearly been spending too much time with my dad."

My attention shifts to the laptop behind her. "Would it be okay if I check my email?"

"Knock yourself out," Skye says. Then she raises a brow at me. "So to speak."

She doesn't move out of the chair or even turn around, just slides a little to the left to make room for me to type over her shoulder.

Inbox: zero.

I close it out and return to the bed. Bartholomew has moved. He's now curled up with his back against one of the many pillows behind me. Bartholomew would make a very good spy, with stealth moves like that.

"Look, I like to joke around, but I'm also a good friend." Skye twirls her chair to face me straight-on. "And friends don't let friends dump lunch trays on people. So spill."

Where to even begin? Someone like Skye—so cool and with a table full of friends—is never going to understand what it's like to be at a mean kid's mercy.

"Remember how I had a black eye when we first met?"

"Vaguely," Skye says. "It was only like four days ago. Wait, that was a black eye?"

"Courtesy of Marc Ruffnagle."

"Ew." Skye shudders. "Decorate his hair with mashed potatoes. Fine by me."

I shake my head. "I should not have done that. He'll never let me off the hook now."

"Well, you can't be getting in fights at school, that's for sure. This guy's been bothering you?"

"Yeah." It's easier than I ever imagined to tell Skye everything. The name-calling, the teasing, the pushing and shoving, the punch. My overall close acquaintance with the hallway tile. Maybe it's the rainbow walls or the fluffy pillows or smell of cinnamon that makes this feel like an imaginary place, removed from the real world.

"That sucks," Skye says. "What a jerk."

That about sums it up.

"What do the grown-ups say?"

"We can't tell my mom," I rush to add. "She'll just worry."

Skye tips her head back and gazes at the textured ceiling. "I don't know much, but I know that when you're getting knocked around on the regular, it's time to tell the grown-ups."

"I told my dad."

Skye looks at me. "And?"

A trickle of reality sneaks into this magical place. "I tried to follow his advice at first, but now—since the punch, I mean—I haven't heard from him. He's out there, somewhere. I wish I knew where."

"Doesn't your mom know?"

A heat like the sun pours through me. "Maybe. But she wants to keep us apart."

"So, let's try something else." Skye swivels her chair to face her computer. "My mom does research for a living. We have all kinds of databases." She fires something up, and the screen fills with a lot of search fields. "What's his whole name?"

"James Patrick Keene. People call him JP." That sounds nice and casual, like I know him and we hang out.

Skye's fingers skitter over the keys. I scoot to the edge of the bed to watch.

"Here is a possible one," she says. "Some guy called James P. Keene has written a bunch of research articles about wind energy. And here's one who's a lawyer. Does the Patrick have a *k*? Because Jim Patric Keene is suing his insurance carrier. And this guy works in Denver at a pharmaceutical company. What does your dad do?"

"Not sure. The only thing Mom ever said is that he had a lot of odd jobs." It doesn't feel right to remind Skye about his spy work. She thought I was doing improv when I said it before.

"There's also a JP Keene out of Washington."

"Washington, DC?" Home of the US Government.

"Yeah."

The screen is full of a lot of small print in rows. I squint to try to find what Skye is seeing. "Where?"

"Here." She points. "All these are the people with his same name. That's the DC one."

My pulse picks up. "Is that a business address?"

"And phone number." Skye whips out her cell phone. Lightning quick, she taps out the numbers, then holds it out to me. "Care to do the honors?"

Do fingertips sweat? The pad of my finger hovers over the screen. An unexpected moment of truth. *Send.*

The phone rings three times, then it clicks. Someone's answered!

"You have reached JP Keene. I'm currently out of the country and unable to take your call. Please leave a message."

Beep. Then there's silence. This is the part where I'm supposed to say something. My racing thoughts struggle to find a path to my mouth.

After a few beats, Skye pipes up, affecting her fakey adult voice. "JP? Hi, this is Skye Donaldson. I'm calling on behalf of . . . a friend, who has some important business to discuss with you." She recites her phone number. "Please give us a call back at your earliest convenience. Thanks ever so."

Skye punches out of the call. "Way to clam up," she says.

"Thanks." I can breathe now. There's too much to say, I didn't know where to begin. Far too much behind us and between us. And an unknown something stretching out in front of us. JP Keene. To hear his voice, to imagine him recording that message, to imagine him calling me back. Or, calling Skye back . . .

"You'll tell me right away when he calls back?" I ask.

"Are you kidding?" she cries. "This is what three-way calling was made for. I will patch you in stat."

Skye's mattress easily cradles the weight of me. Bartholomew lifts his head as the surface shifts, then he settles back down. He has the right idea. Hip first, then elbow, shoulder, and finally my cheek meets the plush softness of Skye's comforter. Close my eyes. Breathe. Some of the ache I've been carrying since last night is lifted. We've made contact. Dad is still out there.

One minute of relief is all there's time for, apparently.

"Up and at 'em, lazybones," Skye says. "We gotta go."

"Go?"

"Our parents are expecting to pick us up from the bowling alley," she reminds me. "Not to mention Amanda. If we're not there, they'll be worried."

WORKING THE CLUES

Among the weirdest things I've ever done: walking back to school to get on the bus home. Skye asks for my locker combination, so she can go in and get my jacket and bag. We don't know what happened after I left the cafeteria, but the last thing I need on a Friday afternoon is to get detained by school officials.

"I think we should go back to the mall," Skye says. "The past clues led us there, and that's where we got off track. So that's where we should pick up, right?"

"Makes sense to me," I agree.

"Except, you promised me laser tag today, too," Skye reminds me. "I've never played."

"It doesn't start until four," I say. "We have time."

"Okay, so let's work on the clues," Skye suggests. "Maybe we can still solve it. What is the last one again?"

> Approaching now is an uncommon event
> Remember the names and follow the scent
> Toward troubling games, a treasure to loot
> Only teamwork can tackle the plan afoot

Standing outside the bowling alley, we are returning to the scene of the crime. The shattered glass at the E-Z Check Cashing has been swept away, and a piece of plywood is in its place. Surprisingly, the shop is open. I guess they had replacement cash delivered. Chet is back at his usual post, in his cage. It's just a little harder to see him from all angles. I try not to look at the dumpsters, at the spot where we were tied up and left behind.

Suddenly, I don't feel like going over to the mall. My stomach feels tight. "Can we do the clues a different time?"

"Sure." Skye's expression is equally stark. It feels more real now. The way we faced down armed robbers like total fools. When we did it, I thought Dad's life was on the line. And Skye thought it was an elaborate part of Christopher's game. In reality, we're lucky to be alive.

"Teach me the claw game," Skye says when we get inside. We drop our bags in Amanda's office, then Skye bounces into the arcade, leaving me no choice.

Returning to the scene of yet another crime. The corner between the Bling King and the change machine is painted with the shadow of my encounter with Marc Ruffles-have-ridges. It's hard to believe that was only one week ago, and that this will be my first time back in the arena since it happened. Pride comes before a fall, isn't that the saying? This week has felt like an eternity.

"Come on. I'm really excited," Skye says. "Show me the mooooooves!"

"You can't be flapping around," I say. "Patient and steady."

Skye stiffens comically and tosses me a salute. "Yes, sir."

I stand in the spot where Marc threw me and try to forget everything that's happened. To forget the crack of his knuckles against my cheek, the whoosh of the breath it knocked out of me. To forget the smell of this ratty old carpet and the odor of floor wax from school. To forget the satisfying smack of gravy, or the way my lunch tray slid right out of my hands. Here and now, I want to forget that there is such a thing as consequences. But standing up to Marc Ruff-sketch always comes at a cost.

It's going to take Skye more than an afternoon to master the Bling King, and soon enough it's time to suit up for laser tag. Skye runs to the bathroom and I sneak a moment alone in Amanda's office. The phone number is still fresh in my mind, but I pull Skye's phone out of her backpack anyway. Just to look. The screen is locked, but it shows no missed calls. No voice mail.

Amanda's desk phone is large and old-fashioned. The handset rests on the cradle. I dial.

The machine picks up, and I hang up quickly. I don't have the words yet. I should know what to say, after all our emails, but somehow I don't. Somehow, it's different. Especially if there's a chance . . .

My brain tries to draw me backward, to last night at home, with Mom. In the quiet of the office there is nothing to observe, nothing to distract me, nothing to help me hold on to what I have known. The question I can't let myself ask swims toward the surface.

"Let's go, let's go!" Skye bursts in and grabs my arm. "Ralph says now or never."

Distraction. Breathe. No arriving late this time, because Skye has never played. She has to hear all the rules.

We end up on the blue team. Skye chooses the handle SKYWRD.

Skye points up at the leaderboard. "CHESTY. Is that you?"

"Yeah."

"Wow, you're like a Jedi master."

"I have exactly one skill," I mutter. "I'm no Jedi."

Skye gives me side-eye. "Don't be such a grump. This is gonna be awesome." She holds up her laser tag gun. "Pew-pew."

I sigh. "That's not what they sound like."

"What do they sound like? OH, WAIT, I'm about to find out." Skye sticks her face in mine. "It's on, bro."

"You know we're on the same team, right?"

"Sure," she says, eyeing our competition. "We can take these jokers, though, right?"

We can indeed. My mind is barely on the game, though. I'm just going through the laser tag motions. At first. Then the power of the arena takes over. We move into the haze, Skye following close at my hip. The smell of the fog and the familiar glow of the blacklights wash over me, bringing me home.

It's been one unbelievable week. Nothing has come full circle, and calm is a long way off. But a few good games could be a start in the right direction. "Follow me," I whisper to Skye. "We got this."

After the first game, our team is up. "THUNDR and CHIKIN must be good," Skye comments. She studies the leaderboard. She grins like she's having the time of her life.

"THUNDR is. CHIKIN chose his name well, shall we say?"

"What does that mean?"

"He's, like, seven. No sense of sportsmanship."

"You're upset." Skye states it like a fact, leaving no room to argue.

"I'm fine."

Skye shoots me a suspicious side-eye. "You say that too much. Do you have stock in that word?"

The arena doors open for game two. Fog machine smoke billows out at us, calling to me.

"Let's do this," Skye says. "Move out."

We storm the citadel, picking off our enemies with ease. Here in the dark, with our fake guns, we dominate. No one can touch us. If only it could be that way in the real world.

Because the fact is, laser tag with Skye at my side is epic. Or it would be, if I could shake this nagging fear. It's heavy on my back, like a cape.

THE ROADHOUSE

"Do they have laser tag on Saturday?" Skye asks. She's glowing with the exhilaration as we pack up our schoolbags at five-thirty.

"Yup. All weekend."

"We have to come back tomorrow!" she exclaims. "We can work the clues and then snag a couple of games afterward."

It's been a while since I played on a day other than Friday. But I would never say no to laser tag.

Skye shoulders her backpack. "Tomorrow. Saturday. You. Me. This mall. Noon p.m. Capisce?"

"You don't need to say 'noon p.m.' *Noon* means p.m."

"Whatever. Are you meeting me or not?"

"In fact, technically, noon is neither a.m. nor p.m.

A.m. means before noon, and *p.m.* means after noon. But noon itself is just noon."

Skye squeezes my cheeks. "Oh my god. You are so much work."

Sigh. "Yes, I will go to the mall with you."

"Aiiight." Skye pumps her fist as we emerge from Amanda's office.

Christopher and Mom show up together to pick us up. They walk in holding hands. This is weird. I mean, I've seen them holding hands a million times, but always at home. Not out in the world, like people.

"They're so weird," Skye says.

"Exactly what I was thinking."

"Hey, kids." Christopher is overly cheerful under the circumstances.

"Hey," we chorus.

"Let's go out to dinner. The four of us. We have some things to discuss."

"To the Roadhouse?" Skye asks.

A known spy hangout. The thought echoes, before I remind myself that Skye was just kidding around when she said that.

"Sure, if you like," Christopher says. "I was thinking someplace fancier."

Eating out at all is fancy for Mom and me. But she's smiling up at Christopher with this goofy look on her face and somehow I know that everything I take for granted in the world is about to change.

She kisses my face and then absently rubs away the lip gloss mark. It's almost like she's forgotten that we're mad at each other.

"The Roadhouse," I say.

Skye backs me up. "Yeah, we like the Roadhouse."

Christopher shrugs. "Then the Roadhouse it is. Tallyho!"

Tallyho? He sounds like an old-fashioned cartoon.

We go in the back side of the mall, to avoid the clock woman. No one says anything about the slight detour. Mom just leads the way and we all follow.

It's a longer walk, going this way. The side escalator spits us out on the second-floor landing right beside The Game's A Foot. Larger-than-life-size stuffed animals sport larger-than-life-size trendy sneakers. Or maybe it's just the hockey-playing owl that's larger than life-size. The giraffe in the basketball jersey is probably about right. The rhino wears a black-and-white striped referee's jersey, while the zebra wears a football helmet and uniform. I've always thought it should be the other way around.

A floral cloud emanates from Uncommon Scents. A banner over the door advertises *Special Event Saturday: Victorian Garden featuring new bouquets "Scents and Sensibility," "Jane Air," and "Pride and Pear Juice."* If any of those smells like the wall of perfume that attacks passersby, then . . . no, thank you.

The Roadhouse diner is hopping, but not overcrowded. We're ahead of the dinner rush.

Skye and I claim the side of the booth that's facing the door. Basic spycraft. Every time someone new comes in, my attention snaps briefly to the door. In spite of myself, I'm still hoping, maybe . . .

A big platter of burger and fries could be sufficient to distract me from my vigilance, but I can watch and eat at the same time. No problem.

Christopher says something about new sneakers. My brain kicks into gear. Why now, when my burger is so tasty and I'm only five bites in? I take the sixth bite for symmetry.

Then I kick Skye three times under the table. Lightly enough that she doesn't shout "Hey!" at me and alert the parents. It works.

"I have to go to the bathroom," she says. "Don't let them take away my fries."

"Consider them guarded," Christopher says.

I scoot out of the booth to allow Skye to pass. "As long as I'm up, I should go too."

It's the mall, so there isn't a bathroom in the restaurant. There's a big public one right across the concourse. When I get there, Skye is waiting for me by the water fountain.

"What gives? My fries are gonna get cold."

"They're half cold already," I say. "You're a slow eater."

She smirks. "Guilty."

"Do you have the clues on you?"

Skye whips the little bag out of her back pocket. "You were acting suspicious, so naturally, I brought them."

"Let's see the last one."

```
Approaching now is an uncommon event
Remember the names and follow the scent
Toward troubling games, a treasure to loot
Only teamwork can tackle the plan afoot
```

"I might have cracked it." I point along the concourse toward the relevant shops. Uncommon Scents. The Game's A Foot. Keywords. It seems so obvious in retrospect.

"Oh, wow," Skye says. "How did we miss that? We were right here."

"I don't know," I say. "Stopping a robbery seemed more exciting?"

Skye gazes upon the facades with disdain. "Perfume and sports. Two of my favorite things."

"Yeah," I agree. "Well, there's an Uncommon Scents event, but not until tomorrow."

"The whole clue is a play on words!" Skye exclaims. "What do these stores all have in common?"

"Punny names?"

Skye strokes her chin dramatically, like a TV detective. "Scratch that. Maybe it's about the order. Follow the scent toward troubling games . . ."

We face the athletic shoe store. Everything about it is troubling.

"Only teamwork . . . ," I mumble.

"It took teamwork to get this far," Skye says. "So this clue must require both of us. Like the locker combination needed part of you and part of me."

Maybe. Probably. "Sure."

"Let's go in," Skye says.

I grab her arm. "No. I—" It's hard to explain, but I'm sure of one thing. "It won't be inside the store."

"Why not?"

It's hard to point subtly, so I use my chin to nod toward the security cameras mounted in the corner of the store. "If we took something from in there it could look like we're stealing." There's no way we're going to mall jail again.

"So, what does that leave?" Skye bonks the rhino on the tusk. "These ridiculous guys?"

"Do any of these animals mean anything special to you?" Owl, Rhino, Zebra, Giraffe.

"I'm a cat person," Skye answers. "And the zebra should be the umpire, don't you think?"

"Referee," I say. There's a difference. Not that it matters.

"Tackle means football," Skye says. She strokes the zebra's nose. "Whatcha got for us, boy?"

"Maybe she's a girl," I suggest. "You don't know."

Skye traces the zebra's mane with her fingers. "First female zebra in the NFL? I'd pay good money to see that on prime time."

In the zebra's rear left cleat, we find it. A small brown envelope tucked in and camouflaged against the zebra's hoof.

The typed card inside reads: *Congratulations!*

Paper-clipped to it are two crisp one-hundred-dollar bills, and a second, folded card. Skye grabs the bills, leaving me holding the cards.

"Two hundred dollars?" I exclaim.

Skye waves the cash at me. "A hundred dollars each. We solved it! Dad always leaves a prize at the end."

I slide the paper clip off the card. "It's not the end, there's one more clue."

But Skye's too busy dancing. She fans herself with the bills. "Why, hello, Mr. Franklin. Won't you introduce me to your friend? Another Mr. Franklin? Pleasure."

We're in the mall concourse, for crying out loud. People are looking. She's such a freak.

The newest card reads:

```
Congrats! You rock!

Such genius for your ages!

Friendship comes first, then many other stages

One task left—choose the perfect finger dressing,

A question to be answered—but only

with your blessing.
```

"Let's go tell them!" Skye turns back toward the restaurant. "Coming?"

I shove the card into my pocket. "Yeah."

Skye dances her way across the hall, barely missing colliding with several people, while dangling one of the hundreds in front of me. "Chester Keene, may I present: Benjamin Franklin. You can call him Mister."

Skye continues conversing with the Mr. Franklins, even after I've plucked mine out of her swirling fingers and tucked it into my pocket. She slides into her seat, cheering in celebration. "We solved it! Code breakers extraordinaire!"

"I see," Christopher says. "And?" He's talking to Skye, but he's looking at me.

"And?" Skye echoes. "It's amazing. The best yet, Dad, really. Super fun." She claps, the Mr. Franklin does his dance.

"I'm glad you feel that way," he says. Our eyes are locked. "How about you, Chester?"

Skye nods, diving back into her fries. "Totally cold," she mumbles. "But totally worth it."

My gaze remains tightly entwined with Christopher's. We don't speak. Maybe I should be saying words, but I have none. A cold wind howls up from the cavern in my center.

Positioned this way, facing the door, it's impossible to miss. The storefront in question is directly across the concourse. A Rock for the Ages. The jewelry store. Glinting and glittering beneath the bright mall lights.

I know what the last clue is about. What the whole scavenger hunt has been about. Christopher wants my blessing?

Mom is watching me with concern on her face. I wonder what she sees when she looks at me. Someone foolish enough to fall for her tricks?

I get it now. This is why she wants to erase Dad from my life. This is why she lied.

Christopher breaks our stare and clears his throat. "Well, what do you say to some ice cream for dessert, kids?"

I don't know why that is the breaking point. I don't know why it suddenly feels like I'm falling into the canyon inside myself, when I've been so good for so long at keeping my footing.

All I know is that suddenly there *is* a list of things I don't like about Christopher.

Number one: He's trying to take the place of my dad.

UNIT 99

My hands are shaking as I press them on the table. "Please excuse me," I say as carefully as I can, trying not to shout above the sound of the wind in my ears. Spies never draw inordinate attention to themselves. Politeness is the path to invisibility. I lost sight of that for a minute, with Marc Ruff-ly-speaking. And I can't go throwing food into Christopher's face. Not if I expect to get out of here without drama.

"Chester?" Mom's voice drifts after me. "You okay? Where are you going?"

"Bathroom," I answer. Two can play at the lying game. "I'm fine."

We've been playing the lying game for a while now, anyway, haven't we?

The sun has mostly set by the time I get outside. The

glowing beehive sign for Honeycomb Storage looms large across the parking lot.

I feel more comfortable out here in the dark, no bright mall lights to illuminate everything that is wrong. Without my backpack, which isn't ideal, and without Skye's presence looming beside me, which is—I'm like a ninja, free of the weight of things. I'm like a shadow, slim and unnoticed.

A hundred dollars in my pocket, and an address in my mind. The lights of the Alexander Street Bridge beckon. Beyond it, a mere mile down the riverside path, is the central train station. The chance to catch a late-night train to DC.

Really, it's not even that late, by grown-up standards. I can get out of here tonight. I'm sure of it.

I pull in a big breath. Blow it out. A good spy remains calm, even when they're nervous. A good spy is observant, always noticing what is going on in their surroundings.

Tonight, there's not much action outside the mall, all of it normal. Cars pulling in and out of parking spaces. People scurrying to and from the buildings. They barely register my presence.

An older man struggles with his cart full of cat litter bags. Normal. If Mom was here, she'd make me stop and help him. But I can't. I'm on a mission. I have to fly under the radar.

A parent hushes a crying child while buckling them into a car seat. Normal.

A short person moves between parked cars, somewhat

parallel to me and a little bit behind me. Perhaps trying to remember where they parked. Normal. Though, when I turn to try to see them, it's as if they disappeared.

A woman crosses the parking lot carrying a couple of bags from the big-box store. Normal. But—

The woman with the bags gets a double take from me. Why? There's something familiar about her. Not Mom. Not Amanda. The silhouette is all wrong.

She crosses under a lamp. The glow doesn't quite reach her face. She's wearing a baseball cap. But the triangle of light is bright enough to help me see—it's Sugar!

A spy should remain chill, especially in the unexpected presence of a Person of Interest. It's possible to be *too* chill, however. I freeze.

Sugar disappears around the edge of the building. I break into a run, hurrying toward the rows of storage units near the base of the bridge. This area seems so weird to me in the daytime, but at night it's extra eerie. Like a series of garage doors with no cars behind them.

But by the time I get to the corner, she's out of sight. The lane is empty. One long stretch of pavement, lined on both sides with units. Each one has a tall metal door and a keypad lock, with a big number painted on it: 85, 87, 89. Evens on one side of the lane, odds on the other.

Small floodlights mounted high on the wall make the lane

much brighter than the parking lot. Signs say 24-HOUR AC-CESS.

The paved lane is big enough for a moving truck to drive through. Probably that's what people do all the time, drive a truck up to the right door and unload their extra junk.

A moving truck, or . . .

"Ninety-nine here we come!" Slim's words from yesterday float back to me.

I tiptoe along the door edges: 95, 97, 99. Stop. Listen.

Sure enough, something's going on behind the door. Muffled voices. Thumping and shuffling.

40

ALEXANDER STREET BRIDGE

Nervous excitement trills through me. The thieves! I step back and consider the dimensions of the garage door. It might be a tight fit, but it could be big enough for the whole armored car. That would explain why they hadn't been caught! Their getaway wasn't really a getaway. The security guards' voices float back to me. *"What do you mean, there's no footage? A whole armored truck doesn't just disappear."* Perhaps they somehow disabled the security cameras and never even left the mall. That's how they did it!

Now . . . what to do?

My mental file of spycraft skills is failing me. I don't have any of my stuff, and the funny thing is, I don't think it'd help anyway. Spies are not cops. We don't make arrests. We watch, we tail, we report. No wonder we failed to stop them the first time. My skill set is all wrong for this kind of thing. And I have a train to catch.

The storage unit door begins creaking upward. Light spills out, and feet appear. Legs. Knees! I press myself back into the recess of door 97, thinking thin. Ninja. Shadow. Stealthy. Unnoticed.

For a long moment, it's too risky to peek. I hold my breath and hope not to be spotted. At least one mystery is solved, though. I sure enough caught a glimpse of the wheels of the armored car. The door creaks again, and lands with a soft thud. A lock clicks into place. Shuffling footsteps echo in the alley, accompanied by a gliding, scratching sound that I can't quite place.

I dare a glance. Sugar is walking away from the storage unit, dressed like a civilian in mostly black. She's pulling a roller-style suitcase and carrying a giant duffel backpack. Probably moving the cash!

A couple more beats, and it feels safe to move. I tiptoe down the alley. At the end of the row, I pause, peering around the corner after the thief. She's headed for the Alexander Street Bridge.

"What are we doing?" Skye says in my ear, nearly causing me to jump out of my skin. She must've been following me this whole time.

"*We* aren't doing anything." I push away from the wall, leaving Skye behind. Or, trying. A shiver of frustration tremors over me. I left the diner alone for a reason, doesn't she get that?

She keeps pace with me, smacking my arm excitedly. "I mean, what are we doing to stop her?"

"Nothing," I answer. "It has nothing to do with us, right?" Maybe I should care about catching Sugar, but I don't. The robbery feels so distant now. Skye's presence reminds me of everything that's happened since. And remembering the truth of the final scavenger hunt clue causes my stomach to lurch. Skye doesn't yet know what I know. "Our clues were always just a game."

The bridge is my destination, too, so it probably looks like I'm still following Sugar.

"We should circle back," Skye says. "We can call the cops and—"

"No," I tell her. The last thing I need is to have to talk to the police again. That will definitely make me miss my train. "It's not our problem anymore."

"Then why are we following her?" Skye whisper-shouts. We huff our way up the bridge incline.

When I don't answer, Skye keeps talking. "You're acting really weird. What is going on?"

"None of your business," I snap. Sugar makes the turn along the path toward the train station. Perhaps I've borrowed a page from her getaway playbook.

"How is it not my business? We're supposed to be a team."

We're no team. We're two people whose parents happen to like each other, so we got stuck together. It's not real. None of this is real.

"Chester?"

"Go back," I tell her. "This is between me and my dad. It has nothing to do with you."

"You can't get rid of me that easily, bro," Skye says, which is entirely the wrong thing to say.

Thunder in my heart, I spin around to face her. "I'm not your brother. Christopher is not my dad. I already have a dad, and I'm going to find him! Leave me ALONE!" My voice rises so much that even Sugar might have heard me, though she's far ahead of us on the path.

Skye moves her mouth in a way that I know means she's gearing up to argue.

"Just stop," I declare. "You're the most annoying person in the entire world!"

She stands very still and her mouth stops moving at all. Her mittened hands hang loosely at her sides—no graceful flailing as she winds up for her next round of words.

I win. I'm free. Sweet victory, but the aftertaste is sour. Walking quickly down the path, with no footsteps behind me, I am heavier, not lighter.

But I forge on. The seed of the idea in my mind has taken full root. I have to find my dad.

ESCAPE TO DC

The train station is bustling. Observation: The travelers look alert and attentive, but unhurried. The commuters rush around barely noticing anything.

The main waiting room is one large atrium, with rows of ancient-looking wooden benches lined across the center. On the far wall there are several ticket counters and a row of ticket machines. Above them, a huge board displays the train schedule, with track numbers and arrival/departure notices. It displays the station time: 6:57 p.m. The next train to DC is set for 7:30 p.m. A relieved breath escapes me. I have plenty of time!

To the far left, the entrance to the tracks. Whenever a new track number clicks into place above, a rush of people get up from the benches and glide out through the archway.

To the far right, a deli, a convenience store, and a couple of fast-food storefronts make up a small food court. People stand in line, or jockey for one of the few tables, or congregate in the plastic waiting room chairs that loop around the atrium.

I spot Sugar in line at the deli. As my gaze sweeps back across the waiting area, I do a double take. Slim is here too! He's already seated on one of the central benches, staring vaguely up at the departure board like everyone else.

A train station rendezvous!

Are the others here too? I shift my route one aisle to the left to avoid walking straight past Slim, keeping my eyes moving all the way.

Observation: Two uniformed police officers are patrolling the station. They stroll casually against the flow of travelers and commuters boarding the trains.

The automated ticket window is my first stop.

A ticket to DC is $88. The Mr. Franklin burning a hole in my pocket seemed like all the money in the world a minute ago. Now it slips away into the machine. Easy come, easy go. Twelve dollars spits back out at me, along with a paper ticket. I lean against the wall beside the ticket machines, trying to think.

Kids my age aren't supposed to travel alone, but a good spy can always find a way to game the system. I've ridden the train before, with Mom, so I have an idea of how it works. On a crowded train, it'll be easy. Sit by a grown-up, make conversation. If they ask, say, *My mom is a few rows back. There were no more seats together.* If they offer to swap, say, *Thanks, but I could really use the break from my mom right now.* They'll chuckle. It takes a while for the conductor to come around and get the tickets. They don't even start until after the train is moving. They'll assume you're with the adult you're seated next to, and even if they don't, you're already out of town.

As I'm thinking it through, the third musketeer pops into my peripheral vision. Lady, the buxom version, is sitting in the far corner, away from the food court, near the track entrances.

I scoot away from the wall, trying to blend into the crowd. Three out of four means Ice must be here somewhere too.

My heart speeds up. If he notices me before I find him, things could get interesting.

The crowd moves me in the direction of Lady, which is not where I want to go. I crab my way out of the commuter stream and perch on one of the central benches, six rows away from Slim, whose back is to me. I put my back toward Lady, hunching against the wood.

The train schedule is up on the wall in big letters. It's an old board, not even digital. It makes a satisfying scrolling sound when the top train departs and the rest of the list moves up a line. It's a very nice sound. Soothing.

Several minutes pass before I locate Ice. Maybe he's only just arrived, but suddenly there he is, perched on a bench a few rows in front of Slim.

We've got a full house. My gut clenches. I'm in the right place at the right time, and mad about it. It's 7:05. Twenty-five minutes to my train. I don't have time for this, but . . . a hint of guilt creeps in. After everything they put us through, can I really let them go? What would a good spy do? What would *Dad* do?

The train board rolls. A hundred travelers stand up and move. I use the herd for cover as I move toward the recess beyond the food court, where the restrooms are.

Through a gap in the moving bodies, I catch sight of Ice turning his head toward me. I'm careful to let my gaze slide right past him, as if I don't even notice. But he saw me. I know he did.

There's more space back in this alcove than it seemed like there would be. Water fountains, an old bank of pay telephones with wooden dividers in between. Now most of the phones have been ripped out to make room for device-charging stations. Those booths are occupied. The one with the real telephone is not. That's my spot.

I don't have any coins, but the call I need to make is free anyway.

"Nine-one-one, what's your emergency?" says a pleasant voice.

"The thieves who robbed the E-Z Check Cashing at the mall on Dodge Avenue on Thursday are at the central train station right now."

"Is there a robbery in progress?" the voice asks.

"No, I don't think so. It just looks like they're making their getaway."

"May I have your name, please?"

"Um. I'm Chester. I was a witness. You know, when it happened."

The gentle click-clack of keyboard keys fills the line. "There's a police office in the station. Do you know where it is?"

"Yes."

"All right, why don't you walk on over there, and tell the officers what you saw, okay?"

Ice's cool gaze flashes back in my mind. "I can't be seen talking to the police. The thieves know what I look like. They'll see me, and then they'll get away."

"Stay on the line please," says the voice. There's a pause, then, "How many people are you concerned about?"

"Four." I describe the four thieves, where they're sitting and what they're wearing. From memory. My spy skills are coming in handy after all.

"Wait with me on the phone, all right, Chester? A plainclothes officer will find you."

"No," I blurt out. "I don't want to talk to the cops. I just gave you everything you need to get them."

"Well, in order to—"

I don't wait to hear the rest. The receiver sinks back into

the cradle. I take a deep breath before I head back out to the atrium.

The convenience store sells maps, including one of Washington, DC. It costs four of my twelve remaining dollars. I take a seat on the wooden benches in the center of things, not very near to any of the crew, but definitely in plain view. They're all still in their spots. Perhaps my casual confidence fooled Ice. Perfect spycraft. Dad will be so proud. I can't wait to tell him.

It's 7:13. The train leaves in seventeen minutes. The track will be announced sometime before that. It won't be long now.

Observation: Ice and crew keep their shades on or hats pulled low, quietly munching fast food out of greasy bags like many other people in here. They blend in, possibly better than I do.

Observation: The uniformed police officers nodded to a guy in a newsboy cap and leather jacket who just arrived. The new guy doesn't check the arrivals/departures board or go toward the ticket machine. He carries his satchel too lightly, like it doesn't have much in it. Clues that suggest he might be undercover.

My gaze combs the room. Are there more of them? I don't know. It's 7:16. No track assignment yet.

Observation: A bunch of people are traveling with small

children. They all have a lot of stuff and they all look worried or frazzled. One woman with a bassinet stroller looks awfully calm. She only has the stroller and a purse, and she's just standing there. That's suspicious.

Observation: The uniformed police officers have stopped their circuit around the atrium. They're standing together, over by the track entrance, with their hands on their hips.

The air stills, or crisps, or something in the moments before it happens. It's like the breeze across your palms before a clap. Real, but barely perceptible.

Turns out, I was right about the newsboy cap, I was right about the stroller lady. I missed the others.

The uniforms draw their weapons, holding them down by their thighs, as the undercovers converge on the thieves.

The four leap up, surprised. There's a moment when it seems like there might be a showdown, a shootout, some kind of attempt to escape, but the cops are shockingly smooth. Hands up, the thieves are in custody in a matter of seconds.

The whole station watches the action, transfixed.

The uniforms walk the four thieves out of the station, while the undercovers stand guard over the bags of cash.

Ice glares at me as they pass. But it doesn't matter anymore. They're caught.

A shadow falls over my map.

Uh-oh.

So am I.

MOM

It's Mom.

"Chester, it's over. It's time to go home now." She puts her hand on my shoulder.

I shake it off. "It's not over."

Mom crouches in front of me. "The police caught the robbers," she says brightly. "You and Skye saved the day!"

"No," I say. "I still have a train to catch."

It's like Mom's noticing the paper ticket in my hand for the first time. "What are you talking about, sweetie?" She speaks slowly, like I'm a toddler again.

"I'm not leaving." At least not with her. I slide off the bench.

"We're going home," Mom says firmly. "And we're going to talk. I don't know what got into you, running off like that."

Is it really that hard to understand?

"I'm not listening," I tell her. "I don't care what you say."

"I understand that you're angry with me," Mom says. "You have every right to feel that way."

"So go away, then."

"I'm not going anywhere."

"Well, I am." I stare at the board as if I can will the numbers to turn over. As soon as I know which track to head for, I'm gone.

"Running away isn't going to make anything better," Mom says. "It's not going to make it hurt any less."

Ignore.

"Please try to understand. I was only trying to help when I wrote to you. I said things I thought your dad might say, with a little more of my judgment worked in. Although I don't always have the best judgment, I guess."

My body thrums with a pulse stronger than my heartbeat, from somewhere underneath. Drums at the base of the canyon. "Stop. Talking."

Mom's voice goes from cajoling to stern. "Chester Keene, I've had enough of this. You're going to turn around *right now,* and we are getting in that car and going home."

"You can't make me leave."

"Of course I can make you," she snaps. "I'm your mother."

"I'm going to find Dad!" I shout. Whatever control I have left is slipping, slipping. My whole body shakes.

"What?" Mom looks taken aback. I know what that means

now. Her whole head pulls back into her neck, like a pigeon, without the subsequent strut. "Oh, no. Chester—"

"Don't talk to me!" I burst out. "I'm busy." I don't want to hear what she's going to say next.

It's 7:22. The track number hasn't been posted yet. What are they waiting for?

"Honey—"

"No!"

My hands go to my cheeks because I feel like I'm crying. But I'm not. Which is weird. My skin is dry. Not a single tear. Not a drop. I'm totally dry. My hands fall to my sides, useless.

She can't make me. I know perfectly well that she can't lift me anymore. If I just stand here, like a rock, a boulder, a mountain, I can never be moved. It's 7:23. My train will be boarding soon.

Mom sighs. "You're in a state."

I'm full of a feeling I've never had before. I don't know what to call it. The inside of me is burning, like there is a fire in my soul that's sending up smoke, pumping it into a space with no windows. The smoke pounds my skin looking for a way out.

"You're acting like Dad doesn't even exist!" I exclaim. "As if he didn't make half of me!"

Mom squeezes her hands together. "I just need you to understand that your father isn't the person you think he is."

"Don't you see? That's why I need to know who he really is. That's why I have to find him."

"Ches—"

"The man who sends me presents every six months is out there, somewhere!" I shout. "He cares about me. He thinks about me. He never forgets my birthday!"

"Of—of course," Mom says. The little stumble in her voice sends a question swirling through me. "But that doesn't make it right to run away."

Maybe it's better not to know. Maybe. But in the end, suspicion wins. "Mom. Don't lie to me."

Mom swallows hard. "I won't, Chester." She says nothing more.

Maybe it's better not to know. But I need to know. My knees turn to jelly, and suddenly I'm not standing up anymore.

You're acting like Dad doesn't even exist. My own words float back to me, and Mom's.

Your father isn't the person you think he is.

Your father doesn't check that email anymore.

I grip the hard edge of the wooden bench. "He sends me those presents," I whisper. "On my birthday, and Christmas. Doesn't he?"

Mom hesitates. "Honey."

"Don't lie and tell me they're real if they're not."

Mom kneels by the bench. She scoots close until her chest is practically on my knees and she wraps her arms around me.

"Sweetie, can we talk about this a different time? When you're not already so upset?"

Well, that's all the confirmation I need, really.

"What are you saying?" It's not that I didn't hear her. But what she has said is too huge.

"Oh, Chester. I've always wanted you to know how much you are loved," Mom says. "When your father left, you were so little, and you didn't understand. You asked for him every day. So I started giving you small things and saying they were from him."

It's all I can do to breathe.

"Back then, I didn't want you to feel as abandoned as I felt. Now, I need you to understand: He's not coming back. He left—"

"He left YOU," I shout. "He's always been there for me!" Except he hasn't. Why would he? I am clueless and small and apparently very gullible. "He loves me," I choke out. The words waver in the air in front of me, then dissipate like a mirage.

"Chester—"

Betrayal stings like a sunburn, all over me.

"I have a dad," I tell her. "I know I do."

"Of course you do, he's—he's just not in touch right now. He's not coming back. I'm sorry you had to find out like this."

"He never loved me," I whisper. "He really left us. Did he leave because of me?"

"No." Mom squeezes my back. "God, no. Chester, don't think that for a minute. Your father left us because of who he is, not because of who we are."

Despite the cool air, my body flushes with heat. I am no longer a rock or a mountain or a shadow or a ninja. I am a column of steam.

There comes the telltale whirr of the departures board changing. It's 7:25. The 7:30 to Washington, DC, is now boarding on Track 3. A rush of movement ripples across the waiting room. I stand up.

"All this time, I thought he loved me."

"Wherever he is, he does love you. That, I know."

It's impossible to believe her, after everything.

43

THE TRUTH, REDUX

My all-important train ticket drifts to the station floor. There is nothing to say. I stalk away from Mom, out of the station, heading for the bridge. I can walk home from here. Except it is hard to walk. My feet feel like they're dragging through quicksand or made of cement, like one of those dreams where you try to run but you can't, and whatever is behind you is sure to consume you.

Mom follows me. Our car is parked at the curb in front of the train station with its hazards on. A few yards away, Christopher and Skye stand talking to a police officer. Mom puts her hand on my arm and steers me toward the car. My steam self would scream and resist her touch. But my dream-frozen, stumbling-through-quicksand self goes the way she pushes me.

I sit in the backseat, as far from Mom as humanly possible. If she'd let me crawl into the trunk instead, I would. She looks at me in the rearview mirror.

She pokes at her phone for a minute before we pull into traffic. The final puzzle piece clicks into place for me. The grand conspiracy of it all.

○—

It's a short ride from the train station to our apartment. Everything around me looks different. The familiar houses of our neighborhood. The shadows.

"I tried so hard to be perfect for him," I whisper. "And it was all for nothing."

"People make mistakes, Chester. Bad ones. Especially grown-ups. Perfect—it doesn't exist."

Mom pulls into our parking space. I want to leap out and run away from her, but I can't. It's like my whole body is trying to shut down. The path ahead of me—up the stairs, into the apartment, into my bedroom—feels insurmountable.

I drag myself out of the car.

Mom is looking at her phone. We climb the stairs. She unlocks the door.

"Skye says 'See you tomorrow,' plus a lot of heart emojis." Mom holds the phone up, trying to show me. "It's wonderful that you two are getting along."

The idea of having Skye around longer is not very terrible. A small buzz of pleasure zings my spine, but it is one small feeling in the midst of a huge, awful storm.

Mom is different in my eyes now. I don't know how to put things right again.

"It was wrong of me to respond to your emails," Mom says. "These last few weeks, I was trying to end it. I didn't want to be lying to you forever. But . . . it seemed like something you needed last fall. When you were struggling to adjust to the new school. You were so sad, and you wouldn't talk to me, and I was feeling a little bit desperate, I suppose. It was the only way I could reach you."

Mom rambles on. "But I can see now how much I've hurt you. I know how much it came to mean to you. And I'm so sorry, Chester."

"It was all a lie." I fix her with my iciest secret agent glare. "And I don't forgive you." I stomp down the hall to my room. Slam the door.

BETRAYED

It is impossible to sleep when you have been betrayed. All the shadows in the darkness loom overhead like stalactites. Rock icicles formed from years of slow-dripping lies. If I close my eyes they will fall and stab me to death. I'm sure of it.

Mom opens my door without knocking. I slam my eyes shut. Not fast enough. She comes closer. The stalactites fall.

I pull the covers over my head. "Go away. Leave me alone."

She sits on the bed anyway, an enemy agent in my safe house. I make myself a tiny ball under the blankets. The way she rubs my back is not entirely unpleasant.

But I still hate her.

"I just wanted to say good night," Mom says.

I mumble, "Good night."

"Good night, Chester. I love you so much." She says it the real way, which is strange. Her hand on my back is warm. My insides slowly simmer.

She doesn't leave. Maybe she's waiting for me to say *I love you, too*. But I don't have those words. Not even fake ones.

"Go away, please." The *please* is important. She likes it when I'm polite and I'm good at that.

"I—I want to respect your wishes," Mom says. "I do, but I'm very worried about you. You really scared me tonight."

"I'm okay." Steam curls tight inside me, but I won't let it out until she's gone. "You can go."

She still doesn't leave. "We're too good at going it alone, you and I."

"At least nobody messes with your stuff that way." No one is cruel. No one hurts you.

"I suppose. You know, we're never as alone as we think," Mom says. "We have each other, after all."

Do we? I don't know anymore. Nothing is what it once seemed to be. I don't have a dad. My mom has been lying to me forever. My one true friend—or at least my one prospect—was set up to spend time with me. It wasn't even her choice. No one chooses me.

"You don't have to stay," I tell Mom. "You can just leave me like everyone else." It slipped out, through the cracks between my careful words. Steam tends to do that.

"Sweetie, that's not true—"

But it is true. "I don't want you to stay." If she stays, the things I say will get meaner and meaner.

"Chester—"

"You're the worst person in the whole world." The steam is winning. "Get out of my room."

Mom stands up, finally. Too late.

I unfold myself far enough to come up on my elbows. "Go away," I shout. "I hate you!"

THIRTY DAYS

Day one, post-Dad.

I do not come out of my room for breakfast. I do not plan to come out for lunch, either. When I hear Mom go in to use the bathroom, I make a run for the kitchen cabinets.

Goldfish crackers. Fancy juice. A yogurt and half a sausage from the fridge. I can survive a long time on this sustenance.

I don't make it back in time.

Mom emerges from the bathroom and catches me in the hallway. "Good morning, Flash," she says, which would be funny if I didn't hate her.

"You can hide in your room all day if you want, but I expect you to be at the table for dinner."

"Whatever." I slam the door.

The food I took in was not nearly enough. When Mom goes to the bathroom again around noon, I zip out of the room like a laser, a boomerang, a quark. I'll go around the world and back before she even notices.

Crud. Mom is sitting big as life at the table enjoying her lunch. What the heck sound did I hear?

She has prepared a plate for me too. Chicken burger, still warm. French fries from the oven with Parmesan. Twenty-four green peas lined up in a 4x6 grid.

I narrow my eyes at Mom. A worthy adversary if ever there was one. She has weaponized my lunch.

She wants me to sit and eat with her, but I don't have to play this game. All the rules have changed.

"Are you ready to talk about it?" Mom says, as I emerge from dropping my breakfast dishes off in the kitchen.

"I don't see what there is to talk about." *You lied the most terrible lie and everything is different. The end.*

Mom talks anyway. "You were so sad, and so lonely. I—I tried everything, but I couldn't reach you. I just wanted you to have something special."

"It wasn't special. It was a lie." In this apartment there are any number of things that would be excellent to throw. To smash, to shatter in a fit of epic rage. Ceramic coasters. Mom's Mount Rushmore snow globe, which might break even though it's plastic. Faux-fur couch pillows. A vase full of fabric flowers. Come to think of it, nothing around me is real.

It makes me want to break things even more. But that only happens on television, I guess. In real life, I can only stand here, listening to words I'd rather not hear.

"I tried to find a way to stop writing, but I could see how much it meant to you," Mom continues. "You changed, Chester. You were so much happier. I didn't want to see that end."

But it did end.

"I tried to phase it out," Mom says. "But there was no easy way."

You never wanted to be caught.

You were going to lie to me forever.

"I can see now that it was a big mistake. And I've hurt you," she says. I take my plate and go.

My door bangs open—THUD!—against the wall. Skye marches into my bedroom. Unannounced. Uninvited.

"Chester—!" She pauses, like she hit a brick wall. "Wait, what's your middle name?"

Sitting at my desk, I spin around to face her. "Um . . . Antonio?"

"Chester Antonio Keene!" She stands in superhero pose in the middle of my rug. Looking about nine out of ten on the scale of friendly to furious. There's no actual smoke coming out of her ears, or it'd be an eleven.

"What are you doing here?" It hurts to see her, knowing what could have been. If not for our mean old parents.

"You stood me up!" She taps her foot.

"You're like a cartoon," I tell her.

"How come you didn't show?"

Show?

Skye throws up her arms. "Noon p.m., remember?"

Oh. Our mall outing. "I didn't think you would, either."

"Why not? We had a plan, Chester."

"After everything fell apart, I didn't think you'd want to."

"Nothing fell apart, doofus. We solved the puzzle! AND we caught the thieves."

My toes trace circles in the carpet. Circles are pointless. Round and round. No beginning, no end. No exit.

"What are you doing here?" I repeat.

"Your mom let me in."

"I meant, *why* are you here?"

She flops down on the bed with a sigh. "You're a little thicker than you seem, huh?"

Did she come all this way just to call me clueless? She could have done that at school.

"Leave me alone."

"Sorry, that's not in my personality. Annoying people can

be very persistent," she snaps. She taps her toe again and flaps her mittens into an X across her chest.

"I'm sorry I called you annoying," I mumble.

"Whatever." Skye turns up her nose. "I was too busy saving your life to be offended."

"I was fine."

"Fine like wine? Fine like chin hair? Fine like a parking ticket?" She does a little dance and affects a goofy voice, like Inigo Montoya from *The Princess Bride*. "You keep using that word. I do not think it means what you think it means."

I spin away from her to smile in secret.

"Hey." She kicks lightly at the back of my chair. "I'm not done being mad at you yet."

"I'm sorry I stood you up. I kinda forgot we made that plan." My toes touch and separate, touch and separate. "A lot happened after."

"I know." Skye flops onto my bed.

"Anyway, we solved the clues, right? So we're done."

Skye's brow wrinkles. She opens her mouth as if to argue, then closes it again. "If you say so," she says, after a moment.

I didn't plan the lie, it just happened. She didn't see the final clue because she was too busy dancing. No reason she needs to see it now.

"So . . . do you wanna go now?" she says.

I'm confused. "Why would we need to go back?"

"Uhhh, for fun?" Skye says, like it's obvious. "And laser tag."

A faint glimmer of interest tickles my chest. "Oh."

Skye smooths her hand over my bedspread. "Okay, I'm done now."

"Done?" Is she leaving?

"Done being mad at you." She beams. Whatever tension she was carrying dissipates. Her smile is a break in the clouds. Fresh sunshine.

"Just like that?" I say, trying to imagine. The storm in me stretches all the way to the horizon.

"You messed up. You said sorry. I forgive you."

Just like that.

She stands up. "So, you wanna go? We need to get serious about this laser tag situation."

"In what sense?"

"CHIKIN is going down."

In spite of myself, my interest ticks up. "That little punk."

"Between the two of us, we can take him," Skye says.

I like the sound of that. But I'd have to get permission from Mom, which means actually talking to her and that's not really possible right now. I doubt she's in the mood to let me out of her sight anyway, after yesterday.

"I don't know if I can today."

"Rain check. Check!" Skye says, leaping toward the door. But she's not finished. "We also need to talk about the lunch table situation."

"What about it?"

"I have friends who I sit with," she says.

Oh. Is that all? "Don't worry about it," I tell her. "I wasn't expecting you to keep sitting with me."

Skye sighs laboriously. "You are a lot of work, Chester Keene."

"I know." I spin toward my desk, hoping she'll leave before it gets any harder to see her go.

Something soft bops me firmly in the back of the head.

"Hey." I rub the spot as a squawky version of "Dancing in the Street" rises from the carpet behind me.

The culprit is my stuffed unicorn, Gladys Knight. When you squeeze her, she plays Motown.

Skye picks up Gladys Knight and strokes her fur. "Sorry, girl. He had it coming. Cool unicorn."

"Her name is Gladys Knight."

"Gladys! My sister!" Skye raises one of Gladys Knight's hooves and high-fives it.

I laugh. I can't help it. This girl is a total freak.

"Look," she says. "We're friends now, right?"

"Okay," I answer.

"Cool. So, friends sit together at lunch."

"Okay." It's the safest thing to say.

"I like being part of a team. I don't care that Dad tricked us into meeting." She shrugs. "It worked, didn't it?"

No. The trick means it didn't work. How could it? "It's not real," I answer.

245

"We make it real," she says. "Everybody wins."

Without Dad, nothing feels like winning. "Come on down for your one-hundred-dollar prize." My tone is glum.

"You still don't get it." Skye shakes her head, the way girls do sometimes. A way that makes me feel like I really missed the boat on something. She squeezes Gladys Knight—"Endless Love"—and chucks her at me. "The real prize is each other! Chester Antonio Keene, you're stuck with me for good."

She bangs her fist on the doorframe as she waltzes out, leaving me holding the singing unicorn.

46

NOT SO EASY

Skye makes it sound like it should be easy. To forget everything that happened and just move forward. But it's not like that. Not for me.

I'm slow, I guess. Everyone else knows how to shrug things off, while I'm still thinking, *What just happened?*

Mom and Skye and Christopher, they're all ready to keep going. It's like how I'm always the last one to finish eating. Everyone looks at me like *Chester, chew faster!* It's that same feeling. They've already started clearing the table and I'm still trying to digest.

Some things aren't so easy. Like an earthquake that measures somewhere off the Richter scale. Foundations crumble. Or a hurricane, Category Seven. Is anything even left standing?

Day two, post-Dad.

I'm getting better at pretending. That the foundation is solid, that the floodwaters haven't washed away my heart.

Pretending is important. If Mom's going to be crying all the time, there will be no living with her.

"Feeling better, sweetie?" She opens with this over eggs. Scrambled with cheese and a side of cinnamon rolls from the tube with original icing. My favorite. She's even done the thing I do that she hates, which is putting most of the icing on my half of the cinnamon rolls and just a dot of icing on each of hers. The victory is bittersweet. But the cinnamon rolls are perfect.

"I feel fine, Mom." *Fine as a library late fee.*

Day three, post-Dad.

Skye parades past my lunch table, carrying her tray in mittened hands. I never got to the bottom of the mitten thing. That's a shame.

"Chester Antonio," she says. I regret telling her my middle name.

"Uh..."

She jerks her head as if to say *Come this way.* "To my lunch table. We talked about this."

We did?

"Well?" Skye is impatient with me. I'm not sure why. So-cial math is hard.

"Come with me, you goof," she says.

Oh. "You want me to sit with your friends? All those girls?"

"Why don't you think people like you?" Skye says.

"I'm weird," I mumble.

Skye waves her incongruous mittens in my face. "Weirder than me?"

"Apparently."

She sighs. "Just come sit with us, okay? If you hate it you can go back to lone-wolfing it."

She's being too nice. It doesn't compute.

"You don't have to invite me just because our parents are . . . dating." Of course, she doesn't know the whole truth. Christopher's last clue is still my secret.

"OMG. You are so down on yourself. We have to work on that."

"I don't want to go over there."

Skye tilts her head. "You're actually saying no?" Her voice is high and strange, like what is happening is unimaginable. Some-thing not going the way she wants. I wonder what that's like.

"Leave me alone!" My voice is LOUD. People at the nearby tables turn to look at the loner freak. *Maybe now you don't have to be.* The thought bounces through my brain, but it's too small to be believed.

Skye folds her forehead at me. "If you don't want to be friends for real, that's your problem. Sit by yourself if that's what you want. I hope it makes you happy."

She flounces away, cool girl style. It's just as well. There is no such thing as happy.

O—

Day four, post-Dad.

Bowling alone used to be fun. Just me and a ball and ten pins. Now there's a big empty space behind me as I approach the line. No one quipping at me. No one cheering for me, either. If I get a strike, it will feel less than satisfying.

Six frames is all I have in me. I flop into the nearest scooped-plastic chair.

All the lanes are empty. The silence of me not-bowling takes over the whole giant room.

Amanda appears as if from nowhere. She's been watching me.

"Have you talked to her?" she says.

"No."

"You should talk to her."

"That's not what I do."

"I know it can be hard."

Bubble Gum and Bluebell rest side by side in the ball return track. "She doesn't really like me."

"Sweetie, your mom loves you."

Oh. We're talking about Mom? "I thought we were talking about Skye."

Amanda frowns. "You haven't talked to Skye, either?"

"You mean TALK talk, right? With feelings and stuff?"

Amanda's cheeks puff when she smiles. She bumps my shoulder with her fist. "Yes, with feelings and stuff."

"That's not what I do."

Amanda nods thoughtfully. "Your mom is my best friend," she says. "When we first met—"

"A hundred years ago," I fill in.

"Ha ha, mister. When we first met *cough cough* years ago, you know what I used to think?"

"What?"

"Back then I believed that I could never own my own business. Too intimidating. I had no idea where to begin."

"That's silly." Amanda has been running the bowling alley since I was a baby. She knows how to do everything on her own. One time she even patched the bowling alley roof. She climbed right on up there with a bucket of tar. I held the ladder.

"We know that now," she says. "But back then I was scared of everything. Your mom just kept telling me to be brave and try. And when things went wrong, she was always there to help me."

"So?" All of that happened before I was born. Maybe Mom is different now.

"So, you should talk to Skye," Amanda says.

Wait. We're talking about Skye now? I'm confused. "I thought that was a story about how great my mom supposedly is."

"Nah," Amanda says. "You know what friends are good for?"

Amanda is staring at the balls in the track like I have been, so my sudden glare at her means nothing. "Obviously, I don't."

"Helping us do the things that are hard."

"I don't know what that means," I tell her.

Amanda gives me a firm look. "I think you do." She squeezes my shoulder as she stands up and strolls back toward her permanent spot at the desk.

Grown-ups are weird.

Day six, post-Dad.

Skye does another flyby at my lunch table. Mittens and all. "You don't have to eat with me for lunch, but you're coming over for dinner," she announces. "So there."

"Fine."

"We have to pretend to get along tonight," she says. "For Dad and Cynthia."

"I think we get along great."

Skye pauses. "Well, yeah. Anyway, see you later." She spins

away. Except . . . I want her to stay. I want us to talk about stuff. I blow out a small breath. Amanda is usually right about things. Maybe for a change it would be good to say a feeling.

"Hey, Skye?" I rush out the words before she gets too far. "I'm sorry I'm not better."

She frowns. "Better than what?"

"Better at being friends."

Skye rolls her eyes. "Is that what you're worried about? Puh-lease."

Skye loads the dishwasher so I can play with the faucet. Their sink has a really cool sprayer. When I aim it at a dollop of soap in the chili pan, it foams up huge.

We're silent for a long while, doing the cleanup. Dinner went well, I thought. We did all the right things. The grown-ups should suspect nothing.

Skye closes the dishwasher with a definitive clang. "I don't like this silent treatment."

"Uh." Nothing else comes to mind to say.

"We literally took down a gang of thieves together, Chester. That's like blood-oath-level bonding."

"Okay."

Skye grabs me by the shoulders. "I love you, man!"

"Your hands are wet," I inform her.

"Not for long!" She wipes them on my shirtsleeves with a quick, affectionate rhythm.

"You're so gross."

"And you loooove it! Now, you had best start talking," she declares. "We have less than twenty-four hours to strategize CHIKIN's downfall."

My hands reach for the dish towel, like a properly behaved human should. Then I change my mind and turn the water back on.

"Yeah, I think you're right. Revenge is a dish best served WET." I squeeze the spray handle once, releasing a single squirt, straight at Skye's shirt.

"Ohhhhh," she sputters, as a touch of the spray hits her face. "I know you did NOT."

"A little thing called one-upmanship, my friend." Friend. I like the sound of it.

Skye yelps and dives toward me with her damp arms outstretched. I dance out of the kitchen, racing her up toward her bedroom. "I've got a nice juicy hug with your name on it, Chester Keene," she screeches, tearing after me.

Skye has a playroom in addition to her bedroom, so that's where I'm headed. It's excellent. She has her own TV with video games, a karaoke machine, and a very respectable quantity of LEGO bricks. Plus, a giant panda bear that's almost as tall as she is. I scoot straight behind him and duck, using him as a shield. Skye dives on top of us, but poor Pandy takes the brunt of the hug attack. Skye tumbles to the floor, laughing uproariously.

"That," she pants. "Was a good one." She flattens out like a starfish and gazes up at me, grinning. "There's hope for you yet."

—O—

Skye's playroom has three doors: one leads to the hallway and a second leads to the bathroom that sits between Skye's bedroom and the playroom. On the other side of the third door is another bedroom. At the moment it is painted white. The only furniture is a brass daybed and a weird rocking chair.

When Skye shows this room to me, she says, "We can paint it any color you want." That's when I know.

—O—

Mom drives us home, through the winding neighborhood streets. "What do you think it would be like to live in a big house like that?" she asks. Her voice sounds strange. A little lighter than usual, maybe.

"Are you going to marry Christopher?" My spycraft is still pretty good. Maybe asking for my blessing was merely a formality.

Mom clears her throat. "Well, he's asked me to think about living together. That was all he asked, which surprised me a little." She kind of blink-frowns out the windshield. "Maybe he's feeling nervous because his first marriage ended in divorce."

That's not it.

"I don't know," Mom muses. "Some people think living together is a good thing to try before taking the step of marriage. What do you think?"

I'm not going to call him Dad. That's what I think.

"Did he talk to you already?" Mom asks. "I know he wants to talk to you about it, man to man."

Man to man. In the emails, fake-Dad used to talk to me man to man. I don't know what it really means anymore. Maybe it's just a thing Mom says.

Or maybe he's waiting for me.

"No."

"Oh. Well, he will. It's a family decision." Family. The word bounces around in my brain for a while, along with thoughts of the big white bedroom. Laughing with Skye. The really nice kitchen faucet. But the weight of everything that's wrong takes over.

"All the houses in this neighborhood look the same," I say. Tall, with gray stone fronts and lots of windows. "That's weird."

FAMILY COUNSELING

My life has had three phases. Before Dad. During Dad. After Dad.

Before Dad, I was all alone.

During Dad, the world made sense. I'll always be a small person in a big world, but knowing Dad had my back made me feel invincible.

After Dad, well, we're writing it day by day.

Mom stays upbeat, but there's a sadness around her eyes and that's just how it is now. I don't know if it will change.

Forgiveness is a lot to ask.

It is impossible to let go of Dad, even fake Dad. He's been in my heart for so long.

Mom, real Mom, has accidentally become a kind of fake

Mom. The hugeness of the lie is a lot to hold on to, and I don't know how to let it go.

I am a good kid, like I'm supposed to be. I set the table for dinner and I keep my room neat because that's how I like it. I do everything right, and I even smile a lot, but there's a hole in the air beside me. Or maybe I am the hole. I'm just moving through it all the time, carrying it with me, creating a whole different kind of vacuum. A personal bubble that sucks away anything normal.

Day ten, post-Dad.

Mom and I sit on this weird blue couch for family counseling. The doctor says we can call her Sharon. She has a huge cool Afro and the tiniest eyeglasses imaginable. She nods and taps her pen against her lips a lot.

"What was so special about your dad?" Sharon asks me.

"He's not real," I remind her, glancing at Mom. "Why does it matter?"

"He was real to you," Sharon says. "That's important."

"He always knew the right thing to say. Not like me." That sounds good, I guess. Some things it's hard to find words for.

Sharon taps her lips. "And what is it that you want to say, Chester? To your dad, or to your mom?"

I look at Sharon and smile. Put on my best good-kid voice. "Everything is fine."

Mom takes my hand. "You don't have to be fine, Chester. I can tell when you're pretending."

But that is not always true.

"Try again, Chester," Sharon says. "There is nothing you can say that is wrong."

It's easier to say if I don't look right at Mom, but she's always there, out the corner of my eye. "I'm mad at him for leaving and I'm mad at you for faking him."

Mom nods. "That's fair."

Day twelve, post-Dad.

The lunch tray debacle bought me a one-week reprieve from Marc Ruff-night. But nothing lasts forever. I'm on my circuitous route around the cafeteria when I feel his eyes glom onto me. He stands up from his spot and brushes off his hands and climbs off the bench and moves in my direction.

My breathing slows. I have choices now. Stand and fight. Flee and hide. Ignore and suffer. My ears ring with fake-dad advice, and I'm stuck, frozen, as the cafeteria walls close in on me. In the end, I'm saved by a gentle hand on my arm.

"How about today?" Skye says. "Are you joining us?" She's sitting with her friends already. Did I drift toward them on purpose, or is it some kind of providence?

Strength in numbers. "Okay," I answer, releasing a tight breath. "I guess so, yeah." There is no guarantee that a circle of giggling girls will interrupt Marc on his quest to bash my face in, but here's hoping.

Skye rattles off their names, flicking her finger around the circle. "SammyCateZoeySarahJaneEboniKadijaCassandra-CallHerCass." There are eight names but only seven other people. Several minutes later I figure out "Sarah Jane" is one girl, quiet with reddish-blond pigtails. She smiles shyly at me across the table. Cass is the loudest. Eboni has a bun on top of her head. Kadija wears a hijab. Cate and Zoey look almost exactly the same to me, except one has very slightly longer black braids than the other, with beads that clack when she moves. Turns out they're twins, which makes me feel better about confusing their faces. Sammy is the last to finish eating, and her eyes move observantly like mine. She's sitting next to me, and the first one who speaks to me at all after we say hi.

"Chester, it's nice to meet you."

"You too."

Skye's friends are funny. I don't get a word in edgewise, and I don't need to. They carry on an eight-way conversation in which it seems like they're all talking at once and yet always know what the others have said. My mind spins, trying to keep up.

We're still laughing as we part ways and head back to class. Marc Ruff-hewn is the furthest thing from my mind, which is why, after waving to Sammy, I make the careless mistake of stopping in the restroom.

"Your girlfriend can't protect you everywhere, loser."

Day thirteen, post-Dad.

"He has a bruise on his arm," Mom tells Sharon. "And he won't talk about how he got it."

"I see." Sharon turns to me. I say nothing. The bruise is exactly the size and shape of a urinal head, though that's not exactly something I'd like to admit to.

"Did something happen at school?" Mom presses. "Is it the boy who's been bothering you?"

This shouldn't take me by surprise, but it does. "It's weird that you know about everything."

Sharon nods as if she knows about everything too, which she can't possibly.

Mom sighs. "I'm sure he has a lot of pain in his heart, but he's taking it out on you, which just isn't right."

Mom's answer to things is always like that. Dad had tough stuff to say.

The right thing to do is ignore him. No matter how hard it is. That's the only response that works on bullies that doesn't sink you to their level.

Make him believe you're willing to fight him. He'll back down. You'll only have to do it once.

Be a brick wall. He can't knock you down. Nothing he throws at you even makes a dent.

Be a mirror. Whatever he says to you or does to you reflects back and hurts him instead.

It's a mystery to me, still. "All that advice, about how Dad understood me. That was you? It didn't sound like you."

"I knew your dad very well for a long time," Mom says. "I tried to think about what he'd really say."

"Did he beat up bullies?"

Mom looks at Sharon, who does nothing to help.

"Once or twice." Mom hurries to add, "But he wouldn't want you to."

"So." Sharon jumps in. "Your mom was able to give you good advice, through the letters?"

"I guess."

Sharon taps. "Maybe she can continue to help you now, if you talk to her."

My logic brain understands this. But . . . it's just not the same. "I liked advice from Dad because . . ."

"Because . . . ?" Sharon prompts.

"It was nice to think that someone would choose me.

Choose to spend time on me and be nice." Not like Marc. Not like the rest of the world.

"Cynthia?" Sharon says.

Mom scoots close and wraps her arms around me. "Dad left, and I know that hurts, but I choose you, Chester," she says. "I choose you every day."

Day fourteen, post-Dad.

"I think it's gonna happen, don't you?" Skye says, flopping onto my bed. She means us moving in together.

"Probably."

It's Friday, post–laser tag. CHIKIN didn't show, but Skye did. We defeated everybody.

"It'll be good, don't you think?"

I toss myself into my desk chair. "Not really up to me."

Skye settles into an uncharacteristic stillness. "Of course it is," she says softly, toward the ceiling. "Don't you know that yet?"

"Why? They're gonna do whatever they want, right?"

"That's not how things work in a family," Skye says.

It's quiet for a moment.

"Dad told me, you know. About the last clue. I can't believe you didn't tell me!"

"Sorry," I mumble.

Skye rolls to face me. "Are you just being mad for a while, or do you really not like us?"

Well, that's a nice little stab to the gut. She's not even joking. She really wants to know.

"I like you," I say. "Don't worry about it."

Skye rolls to face the ceiling again. "I'm paid to worry," she says.

I don't even know what that means. She's so odd.

"You don't have to live with the man, YET," she says. "Every time she says no, he mopes around for days."

It's hard to picture that. Christopher always seems so upbeat, like Skye. "Don't tell your dad, but she's already packing." Mom has been sneakily sorting and boxing in the evenings all week. Our apartment is not very big, but all of a sudden it seems like we have a lot of stuff. She claims it's just some spring cleaning, but I'm suspicious. She wants what comes next, even though she won't admit it.

Usually Skye would go home after laser tag. Not today. Christopher had a late meeting, so Skye is already here and they're both going to be spending the night.

"You'll have to pack too, you know," Skye says, rolling up and diving into my closet in one smooth swoop.

"Yeah." It's strange having her here. There are things in my room that I wouldn't want any girl to know about.

Skye goes straight for one of them.

Maybe sisters are different. Maybe they just know things.

"What's this?" Skye noses around in my closet and grabs the envelope tucked between some sweaters.

"Don't open that," I say. Too late.

Skye riffles through my collection of Dad emails. I can tell she knows what they are even though she's not reading them. "You keep all this stuff?"

"I did. It was from my dad."

Skye lifts out a card. HAPPY BIRTHDAY! it proclaims in bumpy letters. Skye levels the question at me with her eyebrows.

"Every year," I answer.

Skye is confused. "But I thought . . ."

"I know."

The bin of my prized possessions is under my bed. Skye helps me pull it out. All my birthday and Christmas gifts from Dad. A circuit board. The lockpick kit and practice lock. *LEGO: The Book of Everything. The Ultimate Spy Book.*

I used to look at them almost every day.

Skye surveys my treasures. Her expression is appropriately reverent. "This is great stuff," she says. "Really cool."

I put the envelope of letters into the bin and seal it all back up. Shove it away.

"You know, everything he gave you is real," Skye says. "Even though he's not."

My gut tightens, but I hold on to her words.

Everything he gave you is real. She sounds so certain.

Maybe it would be better to never have thought he was there. I'd still miss him, I'm sure, but I wouldn't be losing him.

I tried so hard to get it right. Perfect spy. Perfect son. And for what?

"Are you ever going to forgive her?" Skye asks.

"No," I answer. She can't understand. Everything rolls right off her. When she's mad, she gets loud for five seconds and then it's over.

"Really?"

"I don't know." The no felt harsh and terrible. Part of me likes that and part of me hates it.

"You're looking at this all wrong," Skye says. "You think the clues add up to one thing, but really there's a whole other story."

"What are you talking about?"

Skye shrugs. "If you don't know, I can't tell you."

Day sixteen, post-Dad.

Christopher and Skye have left.

"How's your room coming?" Mom asks. She wants me to look for old toys and clothes I can donate.

"It's done," I answer. Skye and I rocked that situation hard. We make a good team.

"Good work," Mom says.

"I want to know about my dad."

Mom looks up from the papers on the coffee table. She's surrounded by pouches of bills or taxes or something like that. Her expression turns hopeful, like Bartholomew when he's waiting for treats. "You do. What do you want to know?"

I flop into the armchair and wait. Mom pushes a pile of boxes out of the way so she can see me better.

I want to know everything. Everything. But like most things I want, it's impossible.

"He's not a bad person," Mom says. "He just . . . He can't hold still. He has to be moving. He's the opposite of you, in that way." She smiles lightly. "But you're so much like him, too. Smart. Determined. Handsome." She gazes at me with an expression I don't quite understand.

"I look like him?" The photos never made me feel that way.

"Oh, yeah," she says. "Quite a bit. The way you move, your mannerisms. It's striking. Your orderliness."

I raise my eyebrows.

Mom laughs. "He isn't good at cleaning like you, but his mind is very organized. You have that. And he knew how to hold a grudge. You didn't get that from me. I mean—um . . ." She moves her hands over her lap, flustered by what she just said. "I mean—"

"He's stubborn?" I don't know where it comes from, the impulse to let her off the hook.

"Very."

I never thought about that before. Mom's style of mad is like Skye's. Big and fast, and then over.

"Where does he live?"

"I don't know anymore, sweetie." She pauses. "I—I'm willing to try to find out, if you want me to. But I'm afraid it will lead to more disappointment."

"Is he a spy?"

"No," Mom says. "But don't ever doubt how much he loves you."

Everything is in doubt. Absolutely everything. Why doesn't she see that?

"You visit the people you love. That's what people do."

Mom smooths her hands over the paperwork in her lap. "I think that some people have been hurt so much in their lives that they're afraid to be there for others. It takes a lot of courage to show people how much you care."

No courage. So, not only is Dad not a spy, he's entirely the opposite of a spy?

"It scares me, Chester, to think that you might feel hurt in that way too." She shakes her head. "I don't want you to spend your life running from the people who love you."

THE AFTER

For a while after that, I'm thinking about the things Mom said. It's hard not to think about what Skye said, too. I'd like to believe I'm smart enough to figure anything out, but this one is a puzzle. What does it all add up to?

Skye refuses to help me. "You already have everything you need to figure it out," she says. "Right in front of you." She emphasizes the word *right*.

It feels like she's talking in code, and I have yet to crack it. As I mull it over, the important word echoes strangely. Right. Right. Write?

Reluctantly, I pull out all the emails from "Dad." Count them. Twenty-six messages in total. I haven't reread them. Not since I found out the truth. But I can't bring myself to destroy them. It turns out it's really hard to destroy your prized possessions, even when they are tainted.

The words are familiar, some letters more than others. My favorites. The way I used to feel when I would read them . . . it's not the same now, but I remember it. The pages are infused with positivity, strength, and love. They used to make me feel like I was invincible. Because Dad loved me.

Loves me. Because I can still feel it, when I read the emails.

"Dad" loves me. Which is to say, Mom does.

In those words, I can see what she was trying to do all along. I can see myself swimming in a mix of sadness and excitement, a parallel universe—one where I'm not mad and aching, one where Dad is still real and everyone is innocent. The feeling is so strong. The parallel universe almost takes over, but my mad is pretty big too.

Skye is right. The letters tell the story.

And it's not a story about how Dad really left us. It's a story about how much Mom loves me. How huge and wonderful a person she is, and how she tried to give me everything, even the impossible.

Day twenty, post-Dad.

This time, I approach Marc Ruff-life on my terms. Maybe

there's something to catching him off guard and making him know how it feels to be ambushed.

He's with his friends. Embarrassing him publicly is probably not the best tactic, but I don't exactly want to get him alone, either. End of lunchtime seems like the best time. He dumps his tray in the window and goes to catch up with his friends.

"Marc?" I intercept him. "Can I talk to you for a second?"

He glances around, confused. "Um . . ." His friends have moved on ahead.

I pull myself up as tall as I can. "Look, I don't know who hurt you," I say. "But I don't think it really makes you feel better to take it out on me. So, I'd like you to stop."

Marc barks a laugh. "Nice try, loser." He sweeps his arm at me, to push me aside or knock me over. I put up my hands and catch his arm. Hold it tight, using all my weight to press back against his momentum.

It's all I can do to look him in the eye. "I just want you to know that I'm learning how to box. I have a really great teacher. But I'd rather not fight." I let go of his arm. "By the way, if you ever come back to the laser tag arena, I can teach you some pretty sweet moves. I'm always there on Fridays."

Marc gapes after me as I walk away. My limbs are shaking like leaves but I hold my head high. Maybe, just maybe . . .

In my heart there's a mix of Dad advice—*act like you're*

not afraid. Act like you're willing to fight him—and Mom advice—*he has a lot of pain in his heart, and he's taking it out on you.*

But, of course, all the advice is Mom advice, really. And today I felt like tackling the impossible.

DAY THIRTY

It has been ten days since I spoke to Marc Ruffnagle. He hasn't bothered me since.

When the impossible starts to seem possible, suddenly the sky is the limit.

MANY OTHER STAGES

Christopher's working in his office at the back of the house when I knock on the door.

"Can I talk to you?"

"Of course." He clicks a couple of buttons, then closes his laptop. "What's up, pal?"

"Remember the scavenger hunt?" I ask.

"The fateful hunt? I have a vague recollection." He smiles, with curiosity behind it.

"When I solved the final clue, it messed me up a little." The folded note in my hand has seen some wear and tear lately.

```
Congrats! You rock!
Such genius for your ages!
Friendship comes first, then many other stages
One task left—choose the perfect finger dressing,
A question to be answered—but only
with your blessing.
```

Christopher nods. "I figured that had something to do with why you were so upset that night at the Roadhouse."

"You know how you were going to propose to Mom at the end?"

"That was the plan, yeah. Once you and Skye helped me pick out a ring."

"How was that going to go? I mean, what were you going to do to propose?"

"I had some creative ideas," Christopher said. "You know I don't like to do anything halfway. But I had hoped that you and Skye would help me figure out the best plan. I wanted us to do it together."

"That would have been cool," I say. "I'm sorry I messed it up."

"You don't have anything to be sorry about, Chester. I meant it when I said I wanted you to feel good about your mom and me moving our relationship forward." He shakes his head. "Anyway, I may have jumped the gun. I'm not sure your mom is ready for the next steps. Every time I try to bring it up, she changes the subject." He offers a sad-but-patient smile. "We can just keep things as they are for a while. Are you good with that?"

"No," I say.

"No?" Christopher echoes.

"Mom wants us to move in with you," I say. "She just wants you to propose first."

Christopher taps his lips softly. "You think so? Have you talked to her about this?"

"She's already secretly sorting stuff and packing," I say. "She has a book of wallpaper and paint colors and she picked out the ones she wants for her craft room and for your bedroom."

"She hasn't said anything to me," Christopher says. "But I did offer that we could redecorate any way she wanted."

My spy skills are still good for something.

"She never married my dad," I explain. "And then he left us. I think she's afraid that could happen again."

"That's a very astute observation," he says. "What do you think I should do?"

"The thing is . . . I've been wondering—" I take a deep breath. "Is it too late?"

"Too late for what?" Christopher leans toward me.

Everything about him—his posture, his expression, the tilt of his head—it all says he's right here. With me. Listening, watching, trying to understand. Wanting to help.

I stick out my hand, to shake.

"To give you my blessing."

SECRET PREPARATIONS

The plan is simple. Skye takes Mom out for a girls' day, and Christopher and I pretend we're doing a guys' day. They come to our apartment and Mom whisks Skye away to get their nails done and have lunch, followed by some gooey romantic movie.

Meanwhile, Christopher extracts a pallet of cardboard boxes from the back of his SUV.

"You sure about this?" he says.

"Let's do it."

We take the boxes into my bedroom and get to work. Thirty minutes later, the movers arrive. They're not *real* movers, just two friends of Christopher's that have a big truck. The real movers will come after Mom says yes. Today, we're just moving my room and a couple of key decorations. Christopher and I box up my stuff and the guys whisk out my furniture. They blast rock and roll from someone's portable speakers. It doesn't take long at all.

At Christopher's house, he treats his friends to pizza and beer (in my case, the incredibly rare lemon-lime soda), and then we hang out downstairs while the painters' crew works upstairs. Guys' day indeed.

My soon-to-be room gets covered in a nice glossy green. Mom and Christopher's bedroom gets a fresh cream coating and the new floor-to-ceiling curtains and matching bedspread that Mom had majorly dog-eared in her favorite catalog. We even splurged on the ridiculous SEVEN matching throw pillows, because Christopher said the finishing touches would be important to make the best impression. Mom's craft room/office gets the wallpaper she wanted on three walls, and a light blue paint on the fourth one. Just for today, we've put in a desk and a chair so the space doesn't look so empty, but there's a furniture catalog with a bow on it right in the middle of the desk.

By the time Skye texts to say they're on their way home, we're ready.

Christopher puts on his tuxedo. I put on my only suit. We meet in the upstairs hallway.

"Looking good," he says.

"Likewise. Are you nervous?" I ask him.

He tugs his collar and glances at me. "Should I be?"

"Nah. We nailed it." We slap five. He goes downstairs to retrieve the bouquet of flowers from the kitchen. I go upstairs to my soon-to-be bedroom, with the tiny square box in my hand.

52

THE PERFECT FINGER DRESSING

Skye squeaks and chirps with excitement as she changes into a pretty dress. She's all the way on the other side of the bathroom door, but I can still hear her. When she bursts through the playroom and into my soon-to-be room she looks nice, but quite unlike herself since she's wearing only one color. The royal-blue dress has a scooped neck and three-quarter sleeves and it looks kind of velvety.

"This is great. Isn't this great? How cool is this?" She disappears back through the bathroom. When she returns, she has a neon-pink scarf, pink tights, and fancy pink floral gloves. That's more like it.

"Can you believe I made it through the whole day without blowing the surprise?" She twirls, causing her dress to flare.

"Frankly, no."

Skye tosses me a dirty look. "It was rhetorical. I'm actually a very good secret keeper."

This, I know.

We have dinner reservations at a fancy place that Mom and I have never been to. I sit on the edge of the bed patiently as Skye leaps around the room some more.

"Shh," I tell her when I hear Mom's and Christopher's voices in the hall. "Stealth time!"

Skye zips her lips with her finger and comes to sit beside me. She takes the perfect, prim and proper pose, hands folded, staring straight ahead. I crack a smile. This is my life now, I realize. It doesn't seem so bad.

"Just a few things to show you up here." Christopher's voice grows loudest as they pass my door. "Think of them as possibilities."

The voices fade again.

"Gah," Skye says. "Why did we have to be hiding this whole time. I want to SEE her see it all!"

"Shh."

They're back. Mom's voice sounds hesitant. "I appreciate all this effort, Christopher, but if I'm being honest—"

"Hold that thought," Christopher says. "Just one more stop." He knocks lightly on the door. The moment of truth. My soon-to-be room is seconds away from becoming my actual room. Or not.

"Come in!" Skye blurts, before I'm ready. I smack her shoulder. "Sorry," she says.

"Come in," I echo.

Christopher opens the door and nudges Mom in ahead of him. "Hi, Ches," she says. Then she takes in the room. My bed and bedding. My dresser. My bookcase and books. My desk. My laundry basket. My posters and drawings. "What's all this?"

"It's a possibility," I say, just like we practiced. "And it can be our new life, if you want it to be."

The ring box is right there in my hand, for all to see. Mom notices it now. Her hand covers her mouth.

"Christopher has a question he'd like to ask you," I say.

Skye slides dramatically off the bed onto her knees. "Actually . . ."

I follow her to the floor, and finish her thought: "We all do." Obviously, Skye was in charge of directing this little scene. It may be a little over-the-top. I toss the ring box past her, to Christopher, who catches it easily. All those Saturdays in the park were good for something, I guess.

He kneels.

"Cynthia Morgan," he says. "I have loved you from the moment I picked you up for our second date. I have wanted to spend the rest of my life with you from the moment I dropped you off after our third. It would be my great honor to share this home and build a family with you. With the blessing and in the presence of our children, I humbly ask: Will you marry me?"

"Yes." Mom places her hands on his cheeks. "Of course, yes!"

Skye cheers. Christopher slides the ring onto Mom's finger, then zooms up and sweeps her into a hug. They kiss.

"Ewww," Skye says after a minute. "Get a room."

"Oh, wait," I say. "They have one." Skye smirks with satisfaction as we slap hands. Clearly I've crossed over to the dark side, if I'm making Skye-style jokes already.

Mom pulls away from Christopher and wipes her tears. She turns to me. "You're okay with this, Chester? Really?"

"Of course he is," Skye shrieks. "Whose idea do you think this was?"

Christopher deftly steers Skye out from between Mom and me. "Let's give them a minute," he says.

"But—"

Suddenly Mom and I are alone in my new bedroom.

"The room looks nice," Mom says. "This is all . . . quite a surprise."

"Do you like it?"

"I love it." She sits down on the bed opposite me. "It'll be a big adjustment for both of us."

I shrug. "Nah. I don't even have to change schools or anything. We hang out with them all the time already."

"I've always wanted you to have a family," Mom says. "I

think that's part of why..." She stops, changes course. "You've always needed something more than I could give. I knew I wasn't enough."

The truth settles over me like a weighted blanket, like the warmth of a hug. "You've always been enough, Mom."

Mom brushes a knuckle across her cheek. "What?" she says, as if she didn't hear me right.

"You've always been enough. I—I just didn't know it. Maybe we both needed to see that better."

Mom rubs my back. "I wanted you to have everything. And there was so much I couldn't give you on my own."

It's obvious what to say next. "You know the guy who was bothering me at school? His name is Marc."

"Okay," Mom says.

"He's not bothering me anymore. And not because of advice from those emails. It was because of something you said."

The hallway floorboards creak. "Shhh," comes a stage whisper from beyond the doorway.

Mom is too busy crying to notice that we have company again.

I smile. "Hey, Mom. Spoiler alert: we're not alone anymore." We may not have everything, but we have more than we used to.

Skye comes bounding back in.

"Ro-Ro, we were supposed to be giving them a minute," Christopher says.

"They had a minute!" Skye exclaims. "I was very patient!"

"Indubitably," I say.

Mom looks at Christopher. "What was wrong with the first date?" she asks. We laugh.

The four-way hug lasts a long, long time.

THE CALLBACK

Skye adjusts her flower crown, then looks at us, side by side in our bathroom mirror. "People are gonna think we're adopted."

"So?" I straighten my bow tie and smooth my vest.

"So, nothing. I'm just saying." Skye's reflection smiles at me. "We're too good-looking to waste time explaining ourselves."

"You think I'm good-looking?"

"Sure," she says. "Those eyes. Those cheeks. Dreamy. You will have many admirers, Chester Keene."

My face reddens. "After the wedding my mom is going to be Cynthia Donaldson. She's excited about it."

"That makes sense."

"I think—" Pulling in air is hard. "I think she wants me to—" The lump in my throat just won't go down.

"Oh, heck no," Skye shrieks. "You can't give up a rockin' cool name like Chester Keene!"

"Yeah?"

"It rolls off the tongue."

"He's still my dad." Even though it's all fake, I can't shake the feeling that he's out there. Saving the world. And loving me.

"I know," Skye says. She reaches over and adjusts the flower pinned to my lapel. "Shall we do this thing?"

"You're right," I tell her. "We do look good."

"Beautiful," Mom says, appearing in the doorway.

Skye claps. "Wow, Cynthia. Stunning." Mom's dress is floor-length white, with lace and flowers and stuff. Her hair curls over her shoulders, looking very fancy. She's wearing a little bit more makeup than usual, and it looks nice too.

We go downstairs, with Amanda helping Mom carry the puffy train part of her dress. Christopher's waiting downstairs. He spent the night at his friend's house. Mom decided everything needed to be traditional—including the groom not seeing the bride before the wedding. And the borrowed and blue thing, which Skye says is very important.

We gather in the foyer behind the kitchen. The backyard is done up with a trellis and flowers, and rows of white chairs. It's not a huge crowd, but it feels like mostly everyone we know is here.

Beyond the sliding doors, Christopher and his friend Tony

stand by the trellis, with Simon up front as the officiant. Music begins. Time to go.

"That's my cue," Skye says, brandishing her basket of flowers. "Break a leg, everyone!"

She bounces forth, sprinkling flower petals and lining our path down the aisle. When she gets to the front, Skye stands by her dad. We broke one tradition—the thing where all the boys are on one side and all the girls on the other. I know exactly where to stand, between Mom and Amanda, because we practiced. I memorized how the yard looks from that spot, all the angles.

Next, it's Amanda's turn. She glides slowly through the line of petals, stepping in time with the slow, lovely music.

Mom steps closer to me and offers me her arm. Technically, I'm the ring bearer, but I'm walking her down the aisle, too.

Behind us, the phone rings in the kitchen. The caterers are clattering around in there, but the sound of Christopher's voice on the answering machine carries to us in the hallway. Then the message, which is even louder.

"Hi . . . I'm trying to reach Skye and Chester. This is, um, this is JP Keene, returning your call."

Mom gasps. Our eyes lock.

Amanda has reached the front. The majestic tones of "Here Comes the Bride" swell from beyond the door. Our cue.

Mom smiles sadly down at me and releases my arm. "It's okay, sweetie. Go ahead. I can wait."

A swirl of many things occurs inside me—a wind, a storm, a whole lot of feelings—but strangely, my stomach no longer feels like a canyon. It could take one minute, or two, to find out if the man on the other end of the line is really my dad, or just some guy with his same name and an occupation that keeps him from returning messages for months. It's not that I don't care anymore, because I do, but today, at this moment, I'm filled with something stronger than the fantasy of Dad.

I tuck my arm into Mom's. "Maybe I'll call him back. We're kinda busy," I say. "Are you ready?"

We walk down the aisle, arm in arm. Mom's trembling a little, and her face says she's feeling the emotion. It's not that easy to balance the ring pillow under these conditions. Now it makes sense why the rings are tied down with satin ribbons.

I take my spot on the bride side, leaving enough space for Mom and her big dress.

Mom is supposed to climb the little steps and join Christopher in front of the officiant. But first, she hugs Amanda and hands her her bouquet. Then she bends down in front of me. Her eyes are perfect little pools. "My handsome boy," she whispers. "I love you so mush." We didn't practice that. But I like it.

I got Mom a wedding gift. Skye said I was supposed to, so I did, even though it seemed silly. But here, on her wedding day, I know what my real present has to be.

I know the truth now. Dad is real to me because Mom

created him. She thought she wasn't enough. But she is. She has built us this whole big, beautiful life, and it's enough. We're enough.

"I choose you too," I tell her. She hugs me tighter than ever.

Behind Mom, Skye pumps her fist, like, YES! Christopher smiles across the altar at me. His face is serene. He doesn't mind the delay, doesn't mind us having our moment. Into Mom's veil I whisper, "I choose *us*."

ACKNOWLEDGMENTS

This book is dedicated to my pandemic buddy, Sammy, who sat by my side as I worked and blessed each manuscript page with her little orange-and-white paws. She was a good friend in a strange time, and I'm grateful. Thank you also to my friends and family for their constant cheer and affection, especially the Dodge/Alexander family, Emily Kokie, Cynthia Smith, and Nicole Valentine. I belong to two amazing collectives of women writer friends who support each other through the challenges of our profession; they know who they are, and their advice is invaluable. Thanks to my colleagues at Vermont College of Fine Arts. My agent, Ginger Knowlton; my editors, Wendy Lamb and Dana Carey; my proofreaders, copyeditors, and everyone behind the scenes at Random House who helps produce and promote my books, including Adrienne Waintraub, Sydney Tillman, and Kristopher Kam.

Meet Caleb and Bobby Gene, two brothers
embarking on a madcap, heartwarming,
one-thing-leads-to-another adventure
in which friendships are forged, loyalties are
tested . . . and miracles just might happen.

the Season of
Styx Malone

"Extraordinary friendships."
—RITA WILLIAMS-GARCIA,
Newbery Honor–winning author

KEKLA MAGOON

TURN THE PAGE TO READ AN EXCERPT.

EXTRA-ORDINARY

Styx Malone didn't believe in miracles, but he was one. Until he came along, there was nothing very special about life in Sutton, Indiana.

Styx came to us like magic—the really, really powerful kind. There was no grand puff of smoke or anything, but he appeared as if from nowhere, right in our very own woods.

Maybe we summoned him, like a superhero responding to a beacon in the night.

Maybe we just plain wanted everything he offered. Adventure. Excitement. The biggest trouble we've ever gotten into in our lives, we got into with Styx Malone.

It wasn't Styx's fault, entirely. And usually I'd be quick to blame a mess like this on Bobby Gene, but no matter how you slice it, this one circles back to me.

It all started the moment I broke the cardinal rule of the Franklin household: Leave well enough alone.

+ + +

It was Independence Day, which might have had something to do with it.

I woke up with the sunrise, like usual. Stretched my hands and feet from my top bunk to the ceiling, like usual. I touched each of the familiar pictures taped there: the Grand Canyon, the Milky Way, Victoria Falls, Table Mountain. Then I rolled onto my belly, dropped my face over the side of the upper bunk and blurted out to Bobby Gene, "I don't care what Dad says. I don't want to be ordinary."

"What?" he said.

I knew he was awake. His eyes were open and blinking up at me. He had his covers pushed down and his socks balled up in his fist. He must've heard me.

"I said, I don't want to be ordinary. I want to be . . . the other thing."

"What other thing?" Bobby Gene said.

I rolled onto my back. "Never mind." I didn't really know what I meant, but it was on my mind because of what happened last night at dinnertime.

Dad got home from his shift at the factory around six, which was normal. He turned on the television, piping through the house the sound of news reports about things that were happening so far from here that they barely seemed real. The reporters were always blabbing on about economics and politics and the constant BREAKING NEWS.

But every once in a while I would see something that made me want to reach through the screen and touch it, you know? Like to get closer to it, or to make it a little bit real. There was a story about dolphins one time. And a feature about a group of kids who sailed a boat around the world. Special things. Things you'd never find in Sutton.

The problem was, Dad was always talking about us being ordinary folks—about how ordinary folks like this and ordinary folks need that. He usually said all this to the TV, but our house isn't that big and his voice is pretty loud so you can always hear him.

Ordinary folks just need to be able to fill the gas tank without it breaking them.

Ordinary folks go to church on Sundays.

Ordinary folks don't care who you've been stepping out with; just pass the dang laws.

(A lot of times he said it more colorful than that, but I'm not allowed to repeat that kind of language.)

I hated this. Hated, hated, hated it. Which is why I thought about it all night and into the morning. And why I vowed that, no matter what it took, I was not going to be so ordinary.

YEARLING

Turning children into readers for more than fifty years.

**Classic and award-winning literature for every shelf.
How many have you checked out?**